The Foxy Hens
Go Bump in the Night

The Foxy Hen books:

The Foxy Hens Go Bump in the Night
Foxy Statehood Hens and Murder Most Fowl
Chik~Lit for Foxy Hens

Coming in 2009:

Two Foxy Holiday Hens and One Big Rooster

Purchase all these books and more at the publisher's website:
http://www.awocbooks.com

The Foxy Hens Go Bump in the Night

Jackie King
Peggy Moss Fielding

Deadly
Niche
Press

Denton Texas

These are works of fiction. Names, characters, places, and incidents are products of the author's imagination or are used fictitiously and are not to be construed as real. Any resemblance to actual events, locales, organizations, or persons, living or dead, is entirely coincidental.

Deadly Niche Press
An imprint of AWOC.COM Publishing
P.O. Box 2819
Denton, TX 76202

The Ghost Who Wouldn't Skedaddle © 2008
by Jacqueline King - All Rights Reserved.

The Legend of Half Hollow Hill © 2008
by Peggy Fielding - All Rights Reserved.

No part of this publication may be reproduced, stored in a retrieval system, or transmitted in any form or by any means, electronic, mechanical, recording or otherwise, without written permission, except in the case of brief quotations embodied in critical articles and reviews.

Manufactured in the United States of America

ISBN: 978-0-937660-13-3

For Our Brothers

LTC James D. Sprague, Sr., U.S. Army, Retired

John Richard Moss

The Ghost Who Wouldn't Skedaddle

Jackie King

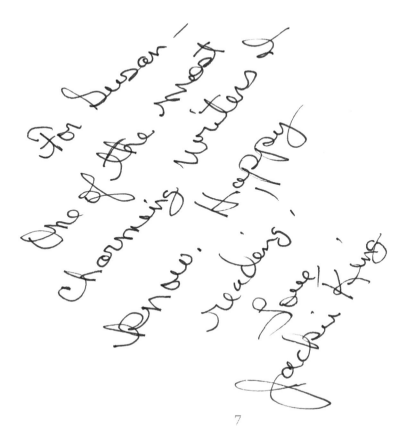

For Susan!
One of the most
charming writers I
know. Happy
readers!
Love,
Jackie King

Chapter One
This Can't Be Happening!
Guthrie, Oklahoma Territory, Thursday June 12, 1890

An ominous foreboding filled Radine Morgan's heart the moment she awoke. Immediately she recognized the heavy weight as a warning from her Angel Mama that danger was near. For want of anything else to call this malaise of soul, Radine had dubbed it *The Bad Feeling*.

"No," she groaned. "Not today! It's my birthday! My eighteenth birthday!" Her first instinct was to snuggle down into her featherbed, pull the counterpane over her head and tightly close her eyes, as a child might do when pretending to be asleep.

"I'm staying in bed today!" she moaned. But of course that was impossible. She sighed and climbed out of bed to face whatever evil might come to pass.

Radine poured water from a large pitcher into the china basin on her wash stand, dropped an old huck towel on the floor and slipped out of her nightgown to begin her usual sponge-bath. The rough texture under her feet and the clean fragrance from Mama's special "beauty" soap made from lye, glycerin and oatmeal was the ideal way to start a morning. She scrubbed her entire body squeaky clean, using a bath rag and the bowl of water.

Another strong wave of dread hit her, disrupting her pleasure in bathing. *The Bad Feeling* wasn't going to give her a minute's peace. She sighed and mentally accepted this unfortunate turn of events.

These special warnings had started after Radine's mother's death and she believed that her Mama's spirit watched over her from another realm. As a child she had learned to heed these warnings, and thus had saved herself from many dangers. Once the strong feeling had come just before the rattle of a deadly diamond back, giving her time to grab a hoe and kill the snake. Another occasion she had instinctively known not to eat the meatloaf offered at a pot-luck church dinner. Everyone else suffered food poisoning and she had been the only person well enough to nurse the others.

Today she had no idea what she was being warned about. There were hardly enough hours in an ordinary day to look after a thriving hotel, keep up the necessary mending and supervise the chambermaid. And of course she had to find time to see the love of her life, Micah Garrett.

Radine's beau was brother-in-law to Harriet Garrett, owner of Grand Hotel, who had married Micah's brother Zachariah a year before. Harriet was Radine's best friend and now was eight months pregnant. Nevertheless Harriet managed to arrange each detail of the huge birthday celebration planned for that afternoon. Every high muckety-muck in town was coming, mostly because Harriet had asked them. The thought of being the center of attention in such company made Radine want to squirm. At the same time, she couldn't help being pleased at the honor.

A year ago Radine had arrived in town with nothing but a change of clothes carried in the bottom of a flour sack. She'd have died on the prairie beside Pa's freshly dug grave if some dancehall girls hadn't happened by on their way to Guthrie's Land Run and given her a ride.

She dried and dressed herself quickly, mentally listing the duties she had to attend to, birthday or not. In spite of all of the excitement, and the heavy weight of *The Bad Feeling*, her thoughts just naturally turned to Micah Garrett and she smiled. The image of her tall, dark and serious beau calmed her anxiety and she felt able to face what lay ahead.

The hotel lobby made a fine setting for the birthday celebration. Radine loved both the fuss and the excitement, momentarily pushing aside the heaviness hidden in her heart. She fingered-waved at Harriet who reclined on a sofa across the way, then wondered if waving, even in a lady-like finger-fluttering way, was considered proper? Harriet smiled back warmly but didn't return the wave. Radine decided that she would ask later about waving etiquette during what Harriet jokingly called their "lady-smithing" lessons.

Zachariah had carried his wife down the stairs from their apartment just an hour ago. Doc Johnson thought she might be expecting twins and had ordered her to neither descend nor climb stairs. She could only stay at the party for two hours and then was to be carried back upstairs to her apartment. Doc Johnson stood behind Harriet as if to be ready in case of a medical emergency.

Radine wore one of Harriet's old gowns that her friend insisted would better suit an unmarried girl. The two women had altered the dress to fit and updated the style. The bustle was now gone. The white silk georgette was drawn up in the back with a sweeping bow.

The bedroom mirror reflected a strikingly beautiful woman so unlike herself that Radine turned away, her heart in her throat. Her first thought was to change back into her usual serviceable shirtwaist and skirt and hide her own beauty. The second was how hurt Harriet would be if she did this. The third and most compelling: *Micah would love this dress.* And he had.

The look on Micah's face when she had walked into the hotel lobby was stunned delight, quickly turning into pure joy. His face radiated pride and adoration. He offered her his arm and they stood together as she greeted her guests, each one remarking on how lovely she looked.

The excitement and Micah's presence along with her tight corset made it almost impossible to swallow a bite from the lovely buffet. Even so, her birthday party was magic. She whispered a sassy remark to him and his answering laugh radiated through her body like the warmth of sunshine. He was the best beau in the world, and just perfect for her. She loved everything about him: his serious but kind face, his dry, quiet sense of humor and most of all his kindness toward all helpless creatures.

She felt his light touch at the small of her back and her smile broadened. He nodded toward nine-year-old Sammy Higgins, an orphan who had wandered into Guthrie about a month before, barefooted and half starved. Sammy was collecting scraps from abandoned luncheon plates to take to Esther, the pig.

"That boy's spoiling Esther something pitiful." Radine's words were mock-severe.

Tender-hearted Micah had seen the boy sleeping in a doorway and offered him a job. In return for sweeping out the lumberyard office and doing chores and running errands for both the yard and for the hotel, he allowed Sammy to sleep at the lumberyard and eat at the hotel. He also gave the lad a whole dollar every month for spending money. The boy considered himself to be rich and in return he worshiped both Micah and Radine.

Micah grinned.

"Sammy's a man who takes his work seriously," he teased. "He spends more time running errands for you, mucking out Esther's pen and conversing with that darned pig than he ever does tidying up at the yard. I think maybe I have some serious competition for your affections."

Radine laughed. "Well, he is a fine-looking young man. I've always had a weakness for freckles and sandy-colored hair that won't stay combed."

Micah's expression changed as he watched her, and even Radine, who had little experience with men, knew he had forgotten all about Sammy and was thinking only of her. She shivered with pleasure.

"Happy eighteenth birthday, Miss Radine," he whispered, gazing into the depth of her eyes. "I have a really important question to ask you later on today when not so many folks are around."

He means to propose! Excitement shivered down Radine's spine, but the thrill was followed by an unexpected hesitancy. Deep inside a frisson of indecision took her breath away and she paused to think through her mixed emotions.

She loved Micah with all of her heart, but she'd also come to love her independence—the freedom provided by being able to earn her own living and the satisfaction of knowing she didn't have to take orders from anyone unless she chose to do so. Radine knew that his question would change her life forever, and that thought caused her some unrest.

Micah, who always seemed to be able to read her moods, looked uncertain.

"Don't you want me to ask?" His voice sounded hurt and bewildered.

"'Course I do." Radine dropped her gaze and studied her well-polished lace-up shoes to hide the tears that suddenly stung her eyes. She chose her words carefully. "I want to hear your question a lot, but would you let me be an independent grown-up woman for awhile before you ask? I don't know why, but I want to experience that for a spell." Finally she was able to lift her head and look into his eyes. His expression, both hurt and disappointed, cut to her heart. She felt torn and didn't know what to say to make things better, so stood mute and miserable as he considered her words with his usual fairness.

"I'm willing to do anything you ask, Radine." His face showed that he understood, but his eyes still reflected the pain of rejection. "I didn't mean to rush you." He glanced around the room as if wanting to change the subject. "Folks sure turned out for your party. You've earned everyone's high regard."

Gratitude for his understanding flowed through Radine like warm honey, but knowing she had hurt him troubled her. Yet she knew she was right to wait, at least for now. She smiled up at him, hoping to soften her earlier rejection a tiny bit.

"I sure am one lucky girl... er... woman. I've got a whole room full of friends." She kept her voice soft and she squeezed his hand, refusing to worry whether or not hand-touching might be considered improper conduct. "And most important, I've got you." The last sentence was barely whispered, but Micah heard and his eyes once again glowed with pleasure.

Radine breathed a sigh of relief and then perused her guests, loving some and liking most. Present were merchants and their wives, farmers in from the country, and even a few army officers posted in Guthrie to help keep the peace.

The hotel cook was sampling a piece of his own cake. He had come from Paris in hopes of free land and had missed the Run by only days, so took a job working for Harriett. The hotel maid, Charity Mudd, sat near the refreshment table in a straight-backed chair, still eating cake and drinking lemonade. Radine hoped she wouldn't make herself sick.

Luther Bingham, a local railway executive who had once courted Harriet, stood across the way deep in conversation with Mortimer Hightower, President of a local bank. Both men were prominent leaders in Guthrie. Other guests crowded here and there and Radine was glad for the presence of each person.

Some of the guests had brought gifts although they had been asked not to. These packages sat on an oak library table about the size of a large desk, placed against one wall. Radine watched two of the men pick up the table and carry it to the center of the room. Everyone's attention turned to the birthday-girl.

"It seems that folks are ready for you to open your presents," Micah said, smiling proudly.

The sight of so many gifts—all of them for her—turned her suddenly shy. She managed to unwrap each package with a proper exclamation of pleasure and thanks. Radine's hunger for reading was well known and Harriet and Zachariah had given her a volume of stories by Edgar Allen Poe, which she had been longing for. Mr. Hightower's gift was a volume of Walt Whitman's controversial *Leaves of Grass* which she would never have expected from someone so important.

Doc's gift was a store-bought lace-edged handkerchief, and Cook presented her with his recipe for baked venison in sherry—a secret he swore he'd never share with anyone. Charity gave her a bookmark shaped like a cross that she had crocheted from bits of string. Sammy had carved her an exact replica of Esther, the pet pig she and Harriet kept in a pen in the alley, and the sight of the tiny hand-crafted wooden animal brought tears to Radine's eyes.

She unwrapped Micah's gift last. He had given her a gold heart-shaped locket on a matching chain, and it was the loveliest thing Radine had ever seen. She knew he must have saved for a long time to buy such an expensive gift.

"I'll treasure this forever," she said, aware that the whole room was listening. What she wanted to say was, "I'll be married wearing this necklace and I'll ask to be buried in it." But such a remark was too personal to speak aloud in public.

Each gift was precious to her and her birthday was perfect—as long as she ignored *The Bad Feeling* that kept trying to slip over her heart like a heavy velvet cloak.

Radine's day ended when the large grandfather clock chimed ten. She walked down the narrow hallway that led from the lobby to a door that opened into the alley. This hall separated her quarters from the kitchen. She checked to make sure the outside door was locked and then peeked into the kitchen to reassure herself that all was ready for the next morning's rush. Then she walked across the hall and into her own tiny home.

The pleasure of having private quarters swept through her as it always did. Harriet had specifically requested that Mr. Joseph Foucart himself design this feature when the new hotel was built from native brick and stone.

She walked through a small sitting room into an even smaller bedroom, and then took a moment to look with appreciation at her comfy bed. Just last week she had sewed the striped blue ticking and stuffed it with fluffy goose down. She had purchased the fabric and feathers with her own money and the fine bed was her pride and joy.

To protect the precious mattress she had placed Pa's old Civil War army blanket between the worn sheet and the mattress. Even a tiny stain on her fine new feather bed would break her heart. She undressed, slipped into her cheap cotton nightgown and sank into the wonderful softness of the feather bed.

The Bad Feeling lightened for the first time all day, almost as if the premonition had grown discouraged from being ignored. Radine closed her eyes and sighed with great pleasure. *My life is perfect. I'm so happy I bet I don't sleep a wink.* Then she slipped into the easy slumber of the young.

Men's voices, loud and harsh, split the night air and awakened her with a start. The steady voice of City Deputy Marshall Ben Daniels gave orders somewhere in the dark and a boy's voice shouted back to him.

Sammy! Was that scamp in trouble? What was he doing outside at this time of night? Radine leapt out of bed as the clock struck midnight. She ran to the door, then turned back to grab a shawl and knot it around her shoulders. If she was going to be Mrs. Micah Garrett someday, she had to act like a lady.

"This man's bleeding like a stuck pig," Deputy Daniels shouted from the alley. "He needs the doctor."

"Take him into the hotel," Sammy's shrill voice answered excitedly. "Miss Radine won't mind a little blood. She ain't scared of nothin'."

Fists pounded on the back door just as Radine unlatched the lock. She hoped Harriet wouldn't try and come downstairs to help. Surely Zachariah wouldn't allow it.

"What happened?" she asked.

"Nick Kelso got a little too lucky at cards," Daniels said. "Slick O'Reilly accused him of cheating so Kelso walked away from the game. O'Reilly followed him into the alley and stabbed him." The lawman looked down the hall. "How close is a bed? We've got to lay this man down before he loses too much blood. Sammy, you run and fetch Doc Johnson quick as you can."

Sammy, his face flushed with excitement, turned and ran.

"Then we're having ourselves a talk, young man," Radine called after him. A boy his age should already be in bed, and she intended to take him down a peg or two.

A man of about twenty-five supported himself against Daniels' shoulder, his face pale under his tan. Blood covered the front of his white shirt and Radine's first thought was involuntary.

Don't put him on my new bed!

The man smiled apologetically as if he could read her thoughts. "I don't want to trouble you, Miss. I fear I went and got myself stabbed and now I'm bleeding right bad. Maybe I could just lay down on the floor for a spell?"

Guilt stabbed Radine. *What's wrong with me? Why am I worrying about my mattress when this young fellow's losing his life's blood?*

She ran into the kitchen and grabbed a fistful of dishtowels then pressed one against the red stain on his shirt.

"Keep this tight against the wound and quit talking. Talking will make you bleed worse. There's a bed right through this door."

He looked down at her and gave a crooked grin. "Thankee kindly, ma'am."

Radine could hear traces of her own father's southern heritage in the man's voice, smooth as molasses and twice as sweet.

"I sure am sorry to be causing you all of this trouble in the middle of the night and disturbing your rest. I oughtn't to have been gambling, no how. It's against the law, and my lady-love wouldn't approve. I just gave in to temptation because I was feeling lucky."

The long speech exhausted him, he gasped for breath and his color faded. He would have collapsed if Deputy Daniels hadn't shifted his own weight to keep him upright.

"I reckon you weren't so lucky after all," Radine snapped. She moved to the other side to help support him. "Didn't I warn you not to talk?"

Together she and the deputy dragged Kelso into her room and lowered him to the bed. The wounded man groaned softly and pressed both hands to his makeshift bandage.

For the first time Radine noticed a gold and ruby ring on the third finger of his right hand. She wasn't surprised to see such a beautiful piece of jewelry worn by an obviously poor man. Many of the southern folks who came west had once been from wealthy families and had been able to hold on to one relic from the past. The Civil War had changed many things. These heirlooms were so dear they were never sold, no matter how dire the circumstances.

The man's eyelids fluttered open to rest on her and his full lips crooked into a lopsided grin that she figured had charmed many a young woman.

"This sure is one fine, soft bed," he said. "I'm beholden to you for letting me rest here. I hope I don't dirty-up anything, ma'am." He slewed his eyes toward the deputy. "You reckon I could bleed to death?"

"Stop talking such foolishness," Radine snapped. "I'm not having some stranger dying on my brand new feather bed."

Kelso smiled the sweetest smile Radine had ever seen. "If I should die, would you give my ring to Miss Cinda Smith? I'd be obliged."

Deputy Daniels straightened and looked down at Kelso with a cold eye. "You walking out with the preacher's daughter? Does he know that?"

Radine ignored the lawman and met her patient's gaze. "Mr. Kelso, I'll be glad to tell Miss Cinda that you've been hurt, but I'll hear no talk of death. I absolutely forbid you to die and ruin my 18th birthday." She had about given up on getting him to stay silent. He was just one of those men who talked. Maybe that was what had attracted the quiet Cinda, whose parents were both taciturn and dour.

"Your birthday is it? And 18? That makes you all grown up. You're a tiny little thing and as cute a lady bug with that red hair and all. I'll bet you have a beau just straining at the bit to marry you."

"I sure do," Radine said, "But if you keep talking you're going to bleed to death from the exertion and pretty little

Cinda's heart will be broken." A quick look of fear shot through Kelso's eyes and she wished she had held her tongue. She hastened to make things better. "Doc will be here in a minute so you save your strength. Old Doc will have you fixed up before you know it."

"I'm hoping not to leave this life just yet," he said. "I want to stay right here in Guthrie. I want to marry Cinda and stay here forever."

His gaze shifted and his impish grin disappeared. He gripped Radine's hand with fingers like steel.

"Who's that woman beside you? I didn't hear anyone walk into the room."

Radine glanced over her shoulder and all she saw was Deputy Daniels' startled look.

"You must be getting a fever," she said. "There's no one else here." She put her hand to his forehead and frowned. "Nope, you're as cool as a cucumber." Suddenly Radine remembered that she had ignored *The Bad Feeling* all day even though it continued to trouble her. She went cold, as if she had swallowed ice. "What does the woman look like?"

"Well, she's right pretty, and kind-looking, too. But she's a little long in the tooth, maybe about forty. She's wearing a pink dress with white cuffs and collar."

Radine's legs grew weak. She stepped sideways with one foot to brace herself. Her heart pounded and her stomach felt woozy.

"Are the cuffs and the collar mended real careful like, so you don't hardly notice?"

"There's some kind of fancy needle work on the collar." Kelso frowned. "And she looks a little like you, now that I study on her."

A lump knotted in Radine's throat and almost choked her.

Mama!

The only time Radine had actually ever *seen* Mama after she had passed away was the night Pa died. She figured her mother had come to usher Pa up to heaven. But why was Mama showing herself to Kelso? That couldn't be good.

The Bad Feeling swept through Radine's chest with a vengeance and settled where her heart should be, heavy as an anvil.

Chapter Two
Friday 13th Early Morning

Radine studied the wounded man's face and considered what to say to calm him. She needed to say something sensible, but how could she explain Mama's ghost? And with the deputy listening? Daniels would think she was daft if she blurted out that the apparition was her Angel-Mama. He might even tell the other men in town and they'd all laugh at her behind her back.

A lady always stays calm and keeps her poise, Harriet had told her once during their lady-smithing lessons. "Giving in to hysteria is the worst error a woman can make. She always regrets such a lapse. When in doubt, say nothing of consequence and be tranquil. If you must converse, the weather is always a safe subject."

Radine had every confidence in Harriet's advice, but she couldn't figure how a comment on the weather was going to help this situation. Finally she decided to pretend that nothing had happened.

"You just rest yourself," Radine crooned as if speaking to a sick child. She removed the makeshift bandage from his chest and tossed it into the nearby wash bowl. Later she would launder and boil the towel and no one would be the wiser. Then she replaced the blood-soaked towel with a clean one.

The back door opened and footsteps sounded. Doc Johnson rushed into the bedroom with Sammy at his heels. The clock chimed the half hour and Radine realized that it was now Friday the thirteenth. She shivered then turned to Sammy.

"I want you to go home and get into bed, young man," she snapped at the boy, who only grinned back at her.

"I ain't tired, honest. You might need someone to fetch and carry." Sammy flashed his winsome smile.

Radine meant to send him packing, but his eager face changed her mind. He'd never sleep even if she bullied him into obeying her. Perhaps a bit of excitement might not be a bad thing. She hid a small smile. *That boy is so like me he could be my own.*

"Very well, but stand back out of the way and don't interfere."

Sammy nodded, scooted back and climbed up on a kitchen chair to get a good view.

Doc opened his black medical bag. "I need you to get this man's shirt off," he said with a glance at Radine.

"You asking a lady to undress me?" Kelso said in a shocked tone.

"Miss Morgan has served as my nurse before and I need her assistance. If you're shy then you'd better get over it." He pulled open Kelso's shirt, removed the bandage and took a minute to examine the wound. "Don't look too serious. There's lots of blood, but that's not a bad thing since the flow has now been stopped by a good nurse."

He shot a quick smile in Radine's direction, warming her heart with his praise. She glanced down at Kelso who looked considerably relieved.

"Some bleeding is good." Doc pulled a spool of gut thread and a small curved needle from his bag, along with a bottle of whiskey. "The blood cleanses the wound so's you don't have to worry about tetanus." He handed the bottle of whiskey to Kelso. "I'm saving my laudanum and chloroform for worse injured patients. You can take a couple of snorts but don't drink it all. I'll need to pour some on the wound to cleanse it." He frowned a minute as if changing his mind about something. "I'm moving him before I sew him up. Radine, scrub the kitchen table with lye soap and Ben, the two of us will get him onto it. And I'll need more light."

The table was scrubbed, the patient moved and Radine snipped Kelso's shirt up both sleeves to the neckline before she peeled it back so Doc could better see the wound.

"You just went and ruined my new shirt," Kelso protested through white lips.

"I'll sew it up for you later," Radine said unsympathetically.

"But then it'll be mended. My other one is mended—I wanted something new—I saved money for a month to get this shirt. Cinda ain't even seen it yet."

"It was already cut where the knife went in. I can mend the shirt with a pretty little embroidery stitch using white silk thread." She glanced down at him with a tiny smile. "I'll make it look custom-sewn so no one will guess it's been mended."

Radine had figured out a fancy stitch to repair garments when Mama died. She didn't want her mother buried in obviously mended cuffs and collar, even though no one would have seen except her and Pa. She was twelve at the time, and clever with a needle.

The thought of her mother caused a familiar ache in her heart. Dear Mama. Radine had been her fifth child, then there'd been two more babies, but she was the only one who had survived to adulthood.

Zachariah walked in carrying a kerosene lamp. "I came to see what the commotion was all about. Took me awhile to get here, first I had to convince Harriet not to come with me." He studied the man lying on the table. "Another fight, huh? That's what I told my wife. She still wanted to come, though, for fear Radine would need help."

"We have everything under control, Zachariah," Radine assured him. "You go on back upstairs. No use everyone losing their sleep."

"You'll need extra light and I can hold this lamp high and steady." He smiled down at Radine's petite form. "You'll be busy helping Doc, and even if Sammy stands on a chair he's not strong enough yet."

"Harriet has no business down here," Doc said. "The party was enough for one day. Carrying one baby is hard, but I heard two distinct heart beats through my stethoscope, so we have twins."

Zachariah gave the Doc same proud grin he always did when the twins were mentioned. Doc shot him a man-to-man congratulatory smile. "We don't want those younguns coming early, now do we?" Then his attention moved back to his patient who had just taken a big gulp of whiskey.

"I feel happier, now," Kelso said, and Doc snatched away the half-empty bottle. Kelso gave Radine a slightly drunken smile.

She grinned back, put a piece of braided rope between his teeth, then took Kelso's hand.

Because of her premonition Radine insisted that Kelso remain in her room through the night. Doc agreed it never hurt to have someone watch a patient following surgery, so it was decided that she would keep vigil on a pallet nearby with Sammy bedded down across the room in case she needed him to send for help.

After settling Kelso comfortably in bed, she stepped back to stand beside Sammy. She figured that Deputy Daniels had some questions to ask and, like the boy, she was curious as a cat. She held a finger to her lips so Sammy would keep quiet.

"You said that it was Slick O'Reilly who stabbed you." Deputy Marshall Daniels leaned forward to hear better. Kelso's voice was weak, but talking was his nature.

"Yes, sir. I'd won some money off of that card sharp then I decided to leave the game whilst ahead. Slick got real mad, but I left anyway. He yelled at me as I walked down the alley. I turned expecting to fight him, but I got knifed." Nick shot a sheepish look at the deputy. "He took me by surprise then ran away. Next thing I knew that boy said he'd get help." He looked up at Radine.

"Miss, I've done things I oughtn't to have done, but only a coward uses a knife on an unarmed man. I thank you kindly for helping me and for giving me your own bed. I want you to know that I'll be your friend for life, or even beyond if necessary."

The Bad Feeling blew through Radine like a cold wind.

Just before dawn Radine stepped into the kitchen and put the bloodied towels into a bucket of cold water to soak. Blood was hard to get out of white things, and she hated the idea of losing good dishtowels to the rag bag. She'd have to check her mother's old recipe book and find her formula for removing such stains if the cold water didn't do the trick.

Sammy came out a few minutes later carrying the chamber pot and grinning impishly.

"Nick could hardly wait for you to step out the door so he could ask me for the pot, then he half filled it." The boy giggled.

"Oh for pity's sake," Radine said. "Why didn't he ask me?" Then a flash of understanding swept through her and she regretted not leaving sooner under some pretext or another. The poor man was embarrassed. She frowned down at the boy's gleeful face, struggling to keep a smile off her own.

"Now empty that pot and don't you be teasing Mr. Kelso about it. It's cruel to embarrass a man when he's abed. You sure wouldn't like it."

Sammy gave the subject a little thought and then his face sobered. "No, ma'am, I reckon I'd be red-faced for a week." He trudged down the hallway toward the indoor toilet. Such a modern facility still seemed miraculous to both Radine and Sammy. Harriet, who had already enjoyed such luxuries in New York City, had insisted on the best for her new hotel. Two of the upstairs rooms even had their own private bathrooms including a tub.

"Don't forget to wash your hands." Who would ever have thought that one day folks would have their privy inside the house? Times were changing so fast that it made a body's head swim.

Radine smiled at the boy's back. She'd never been around young boys before and she found his idea of humor highly amusing. "Feisty outfit," she said under her breath.

Cook was particular about his huge black stove and fussed when anyone else messed with it but Radine wanted coffee and she wasn't afraid of anyone's temper. She lighted the fire that had been built the night before, washed her hands and made coffee. Cook came into the kitchen looking bleary-eyed and cranky. He glanced at Radine and then at the already built fire, rolled his eyes then began lifting large cast-iron pots and skillets to the surface of the stove without saying a word.

Radine knew not to expect conversation from him at this time of morning. The Frenchman consumed a large amount of homemade wine every night before retiring, and she knew it would be midday before he would say anything to anyone except to shout orders at Sammy or the maid, Charity Mudd.

Radine's eyes ached from lack of sleep. She had worried about her patient most of the night, and the hardness of the pallet on the floor made her muscles ache.

Sammy returned as directed and then glanced toward the door. She suspected he was thinking about stepping outside for his morning talk with Esther, something she herself enjoyed doing. Pigs were such intelligent animals. Sometimes it seemed that oinker knew just what she was saying and would be glad to give her a wise and helpful answer if only she could speak English.

"Did you rinse out the chamber pot?" Sammy nodded and grinned. "Then put it back under the bed, and if Mr. Kelso is asleep don't bother him. Breakfast will be ready soon and then he can eat something."

Sammy ran to do her bidding and her thoughts turned to her patient.

Nick Kelso wasn't really handsome, but there was something about him that made a woman look twice: the tilt of his head, the cocky grin, and something indefinable that she couldn't explain.

There had been some gossip about the new man in town. There always was in Guthrie, and Radine had learned to pay little heed to folk's wagging tongues. She knew from personal experience the pain caused by unwarranted gossip. Deserved gossip would sting even worse, she figured. For sure a woman's good name was one of the most important things she had. And since one day she hoped to be Mrs. Micah Garrett, she had his reputation to safeguard, too.

Radine knew her nature was impetuous and blunt. She appreciated Harriet schooling her in ways to better handle social situations, although she wasn't sure that what worked for Harriet would work equally well for her.

"You catch more flies with honey than with vinegar," Harriet had said.

"Why would I want flies?" The remark flew unbidden from Radine's mouth and made Harriet laugh.

Honey seemed false on Radine's tongue if she didn't really feel sweet herself. Vinegar sprang more naturally to her lips. The acid cleansed and preserved, and had been more plentiful on the prairie where she grew up. Honey was precious and sticky, and in Radine's mind should be kept for very special occasions; at least for her.

She forced her mind back to Kelso. Micah had told her that the Postmaster claimed Kelso was 'an inveterate flirt, who shouldn't be trusted,' and Micah had said he agreed. Of course this was after Micah caught her gazing at Kelso for longer than he had liked. She told him that everyone studied other folks at church, and she supposed that had settled the matter.

    Sammy tiptoed back to the kitchen and whispered, "Mr. Kelso's sound asleep, but then he's got a real good bed so I reckon sleeping would be easy." Then, under Radine's directions, the boy made another trip to the bathroom and washed, readying himself for the day. When he came back, he looked at Radine with the innocence of youth.

    "What do you reckon Mr. Micah's going to think about you and me sleeping last night with a jackanapes?"

    "Sammy Higgins! Do you even know what a jackanapes is?" Radine faced him with her hands on her hips and her foot tapping.

    Sammy's eyes blinked in surprise and he took a step backwards. "No ma'am, but it must be something bad. Mr. Micah looked real peeved when he spoke the word about Nick Kelso."

Chapter Three
Friday the Thirteenth Continues

Sammy's words troubled Radine. She thought Mama's warning pertained to physical danger. Could it instead be heralding a serious danger to her happiness? She'd rather face a stampeding herd of wild buffalos than lose Micah's love.

Her beau hadn't come by for breakfast and he always did. She could set her clock by his appearance. A cold chill filled her heart. Sammy, meaning no mischief, no doubt ran immediately to tell Micah of last night's drama. Radine touched the gold heart hanging from her neck. She must tell Micah that Kelso loved Cinda Smith so he wouldn't be jealous but she couldn't leave the hotel at this busy hour.

Radine continued her morning duties. When she was sure Kelso would be awake, she carried in his breakfast, disappointed that Doc hadn't yet come to check him over so he could leave.

"Thank you, Miss Radine." Kelso tucked a napkin under his chin.

She left him eating and hurried to the kitchen to get potato peelings and other scraps for Esther. The couple had fallen into the habit of meeting and chatting in the alley. The pig pen was a perfect spot with very little traffic passing through, yet public enough to be considered socially acceptable.

Micah had been an Ohio farmer before he came to the Land Rush and began working at the lumberyard. She knew he was still a farm-boy at heart and liked to check on the red, droopy-eared Duroc pig.

Radine was about to step out the back door when *The Bad Feeling* stopped her in her tracks. Radine frowned. That settled it. Her premonition wasn't to prevent trouble between Micah and her. If she didn't show at the usual time Micah might think the worst. She had to meet him if only for a minute.

She turned the knob and *The Bad Feeling* grew stronger. Mama seemed to be telling her not to leave Kelso. She paused for a minute and then released the knob and called for Charity. The girl stuck her head out the kitchen door drying her hands on her apron.

"Run outside and ask Micah to come inside for a minute. I'll be in my quarters." Surely it wouldn't hurt for him to visit her there if she left the hall door open.

Radine walked back into her sitting room remembering that it was a year ago when Micah started slipping away from the lumberyard to spend a few precious minutes with her. She likewise made sure that every day at exactly ten o'clock she stepped out to feed Esther. Their conversations had advanced from discussing the fine qualities of pigs to Micah describing her hair as being the exact same color as an Oklahoma Territory sunset.

She wished there was someway to tell Micah about Mama's warnings, but she feared he'd think her loony. She went back into her sitting room and fingered a stack of linen waiting to be inspected for tears. In less than a minute Micah walked into her apartment.

Radine saw him pause with his hand on the door, as if he were considering closing it for privacy. He looked at her and his eyes softened and he pushed it wide open. An unmarried woman, alone in her rooms with a man, would be the scandal of Guthrie.

He cared!

"I'm sure glad to see you. Let me get you like a cup of coffee and something to eat. You didn't show up for breakfast this morning and I'll bet you're hungry."

"I made coffee at the lumberyard," Micah said.

"Don't you even want a biscuit with butter and honey?"

"No," Micah said.

Radine touched the gold locket around her neck. "I really am glad to see you," she said again.

"Are you? I almost didn't come. When Charity came to fetch me I figured that if you were too busy to come outside maybe I ought to go back to work." His expression looked a bit like Sammy's when the boy's feelings had been hurt beyond his endurance.

"Why Micah Garrett, you're jealous!" She could barely keep from smiling.

"Maybe I have reason to be," Micah shot back.

"Of course you don't! I'm only doing what any decent woman would do—looking after the sick and wounded. The poor man was stabbed."

Micah's mouth tightened and his eyes flashed danger signals. Every muscle in his expressive face said, *that's no surprise to me—I'd like to stab the varmint myself.* But his mouth spoke not one word. He just looked at her. Radine's temper almost boiled over, but her fear of spoiling things between them kept her from lashing out. Instead she stepped forward and touched Micah's hand. His eyes softened, but then Kelso called out.

"Miss Radine? I tried to sit up and may have pulled a stitch loose. Could you check my bandage?"

Radine glanced at the bedroom door, then back up at Micah. "I truly am glad you're here, but I'd better see what ails him." Micah's eyes hardened.

"It won't hurt him to bleed a minute. I can't stay long."

"Why Micah, I'm surprised at you."

"Miss Radine, did you hear me?" Kelso said.

A muscle in Micah's jaw tightened. "If you leave me to go to him I won't be here when you get back."

Radine's temper flared. "Micah Garrett, you're acting like a spoiled child!" She pulled open the bedroom door and strode inside, then looked defiantly at Micah.

Micah blanched. He looked so hurt that Radine gasped. Then he turned on the heel of his well polished boot and left.

"Micah!" Radine was so stunned it took a minute for her to react. She shouted and then raced after him. In her haste she left both her apartment door and the hotel door wide open, never giving either a thought.

"Micah Garrett, you come back here. Don't be such a jackass!" she shouted. Micah stopped dead in his tracks and turned to glare at her from the end of the alley. Red splotches flared on his cheeks.

"Jackass? No real lady would ever speak such a coarse word." Then he walked quickly away.

His words hit Radine like a pitcher of ice water thrown in her face. Micah knew of her struggle to better herself—knew she often lapsed back into language she was ashamed of. He had deliberately spoken words that he meant to wound her.

Shock kept her from either thinking or speaking. Her anger disappeared and grief almost consumed her. She stumbled over and leaned against a fence post on Esther's pen.

Hot tears ran down her cheeks. She seldom cried and never in public, but today her eyes turned into artesian springs. She had no more control over her tears than she had over drawing breath. Her legs collapsed and she sat cross-legged facing Esther and wept into her apron.

In that moment nothing mattered. She gave no thought to the picture she might present to curious townsfolk taking a short cut down the alley: a young woman, her face covered with her apron, sitting in the dust and crying her eyes out. Even Esther's soft and sympathetic pig noises didn't penetrate Radine's grief. She just had to cry. Time disappeared.

"Radine?"

A woman's soft, frightened sounding voice brought her back into reality. Radine blinked, snuffled and then quickly dried her eyes with the hem of her apron. But she couldn't speak.

"Whatever is wrong? Have you been injured?" The voice belonged to Emmaline Smith, wife of a new preacher in town. "Please, my dear, you must collect yourself. You can't make yourself a public spectacle—people will talk. A young woman's reputation can so easily be ruined forever, even here in the West." She bent down and helped Radine to stand.

Radine wiped her eyes with her already damp apron and then struggled to arrange her long calico skirt to cover her ankles. She had no idea what to say.

"Fancy meeting you here, Mrs. Smith. I reckon I do look a fright." She wished someone other than the preacher's wife had happened by. No doubt she would tell her husband and then he'd come by, too. The man was underfoot enough already. Almost every day he came to try and get Cook to come to church services.

"I guess I plumb forgot myself," Radine finally said.

"Have you been here long?" Mrs. Smith asked anxiously.

"No," Radine said and then hesitated. "Well...I don't really know...maybe…. I sort of lost track of where I was for awhile."

"Were you crying over a young man?" Mrs. Smith asked gently.

The question took Radine by surprise and she answered truthfully. "I reckon I was. There's this special fellow and I hurt his feelings real bad without meaning to, and then he hurt mine on purpose." Tears stung her eyes and she blinked hard.

"Gentlemen think very differently from young ladies, I have learned. Did he misunderstand about your nursing the young man who was stabbed last night?"

Mrs. Smith's answer surprised her. Radine blinked hard. "How did you hear about that?"

Mrs. Smith smiled. "Gossip travels quickly in Guthrie, and it always comes first to the parsonage. It's so easy to pass tittle-tattle under the pretense of asking for prayer for those who are being slandered."

A sharp retort about a buzzard preying on a wounded bird sprang to Radine's lips, but just before she spoke a gentle breeze touched her cheek—almost like a mother's kiss. It gave her pause, and wiser words came out of her mouth.

"How did you know that? Who told you?"

Mrs. Smith smiled. "The person meant no harm to either you or to the young man."

For the first time Radine really looked at Emmaline Smith. Before, she had seen a drably dressed middle-aged woman bent on helping her husband build a new church in Guthrie. Now she saw the woman herself: intelligent, courageous and kind. Not all that different from Harriet when she and Radine had first met.

It suddenly occurred to Radine that the friendly atmosphere of the new church that had appealed to her, might be due to the force of Mrs. Smith's presence. Perhaps that was what had drawn her to attend, although Micah preferred the more traditional Presbyterian Church. To compromise, the couple had alternated Sundays.

Mrs. Smith inquired after the welfare of Nick Kelso and asked if there was anything she could do for the unfortunate young man.

"Maybe Preacher Smith might drop by and say a few encouraging words to Mr. Kelso?" Radine said.

"I'll mention it to him, dear, but Mr. Smith has been very busy lately, so it may be awhile." The older woman paused for a moment. "I understand that Mr. Kelso isn't in any danger?"

"No, he isn't." Then she remembered Mama's warning. Her gaze shot to the hotel back entrance and her heart froze. The door was open! With a start she remembered she had left it open, as well as her own door.

She quickly said goodbye to Emmaline Smith who continued down the alley.

Radine gathered up her long skirts and ran inside just as the clock chimed eleven from the lobby. She must have cried for at least half an hour! Micah's words had upset her so much she had plumb forgotten about Kelso! How could she have done such a thing? And after Mama's warning! She ran to her bedroom and then stopped dead in her tracks.

Nick Kelso's eyes were open and staring vacantly into space. His soul had passed from this life into the next.

Chapter Four
Things Get Worse

"The man's dead all right," Doc Johnson proclaimed without even touching the patient.

"Tarnation! For sure this is Friday the 13th," Sammy said. The boy had slipped in on the heels of Doc Johnson.

"You oughtn't to be here!" Radine snapped at him to cover her own remorse. Doc's words were no surprise, but she still wanted to put her head down and bawl like a baby.

Sammy's face fell at her sharp words.

"Oh Sammy, I'm sorry I yelled at you. It's my fault Kelso's dead. I left him when I shouldn't have. If I'd stayed with him he'd still be alive."

"You weren't the one who stabbed him," Sammy said loyally.

"He called for help and I didn't go to see about him for almost half an hour."

Doc patted her shoulder. "You couldn't stay with him every minute," he said. "Don't blame yourself. You did your best."

"I knew I should stay," Radine said softly, but Doc was bending over studying Kelso's stab wound and didn't answer. "He said he might have pulled a stitch, but I left. When I came back he was dead." Radine's voice broke. She stood as tall as her five feet would allow and drew a deep breath to steady herself. "I sure am sorry."

"I should have stayed and helped you," Sammy said, seeming determined to share the guilt.

"Neither of you are at fault." Doc's voice sounded grim.

"He asked me to give his ring to Cinda Smith." Touching a dead body was never easy, but she steeled herself and slipped the ring off his finger. Doc had covered Kelso's chest with one of the kitchen towels stacked nearby and Radine reached to pull it away from the wound.

"No need for you to look," Doc said, moving to stop her.

But Radine was young and quick. She stared at the now-stitched cut. "There isn't enough blood for him to have bled to death," she said.

"People die unexpectedly," Doc said, "Sometimes of nothing but shock." He pulled the sheet over Kelso's face. "I'll go tell the undertaker. I reckon young Kelso will need the town of Guthrie to pay for his burial."

"A pauper's grave?" Radine hated the thought. The shame of an indigent burial didn't seem right, Kelso deserved better. "I can hammer together a wooden cross," she said feeling the offer was lame at best.

"I'll carve his name and the year on it," Sammy said. "And I know where there's a patch of wildflowers. They'll look real pretty sprinkled on the grave."

"Maybe Pastor Smith would say a few words over him," she said, wishing she could have done more for Nick Kelso.

Radine walked to the parsonage as soon as she could manage to get away from her hotel duties. Sammy had been summoned to the lumberyard to sort nails from some broken kegs just unloaded off the freight train, so she went alone. Luckily she found both the preacher and his wife at home.

"I thought he was going to be all right," Mrs. Smith said, looking paler than she had in the alley. "He was so young." Her voice broke.

"There, there, my dear," Pastor patted her hand. "We are all fragile creatures." He turned to Radine. "Mrs. Smith is very tender hearted, you see. She feels things more deeply than most people."

"I was wondering if you would say a few words at his funeral, Pastor?" Radine said.

Before he could respond his wife answered for him in a clear voice. "Of course Mr. Smith will deliver the service. It's the Christian thing to do."

"I sure do appreciate that." Radine glanced at the pastor, and saw uncertainty in his face.

"It's always hard to eulogize someone you don't know," Pastor said with hesitation.

"No one is more adept with words than you," Mrs. Smith said. "I'll help by choosing a few comforting hymns. We should have a short service in the sanctuary before going to the cemetery."

It was much more than Radine expected and she saw Pastor Smith was also surprised at his wife's offer, but he accepted graciously.

"Thank you both," Radine said.

The next day Zachariah rented a carriage to drive everyone to the funeral. Radine's heart sank when he arrived with only a well-scrubbed Sammy beside him.

"Micah wasn't able to get away from the yard," Zachariah said avoiding Radine's eyes. Sammy reached for her hand and held it with a worried look on his face.

Radine longed for Harriet's presence, but Doc had ordered her to stay home. Radine hadn't discussed their tiff with Harriet because it seemed unfair to make her choose sides between her brother-in-law and her best friend.

Sammy ran to hold the horses steady while Zachariah stepped down to assist the ladies.

How Radine wished that Micah was there. Even the slightest touch of his hand would be welcomed. A sickness of heart washed through her. Would Micah ever forgive her for choosing Kelso over him? She touched her locket. Never had she thought anything could cause a rift between them but Micah was a proud man, and loyalty meant everything to him. He loved her, but he also expected her love for him to be just as strong. They had discussed how hard life could be on the frontier and how important it was to have a spouse you could totally depend upon. Had he decided to find someone he could trust more?

She watched Cook and Charity climb into the back seat dressed in their Sunday best. Each had insisted that it was their duty to come. After all, Kelso had died across from the kitchen. Radine sat in the front of the carriage with Sammy and Zachariah. She thought of Micah all the way to the church.

Radine was surprised to see so many people inside, including a number of church members. Those folks had no doubt come out of habit, thinking it was their duty to be present whenever the doors opened. Her group slid into the next to last pew where there was room for all of them.

Sammy led the way, his small warm hand still holding hers, and his touch was a great comfort.

They passed Deputy Daniels standing at the back of the room. Pastor Smith was seated on the dais with Bible in hand. Emmaline sat at the piano and Cinda was in the first pew twisting a white lace handkerchief. Radine pitied the girl, hoping her heart would soon mend. Doc Johnson sat next to her.

Also surprising was the banker Mortimer Hightower sitting in a middle pew. But most astonishing of all, the railroad executive Luther Bingham, sat just across the aisle. What on earth was *he* doing here? Radine studied the back of his head and wished she could see his face. What had brought him?

Radine's gaze fell to the casket and she caught her breath. The box wasn't rough pine as she had expected but real walnut. Nick Kelso couldn't have had enough money to pay for such a thing. The man had saved to buy a new shirt! His only treasure, the gold and ruby ring, was tied onto a loop of ribbon tucked inside her reticule. Could Hightower or Bingham have provided such a fine box? And if so, why?

Also present, but more to be expected, was the owner of the Emporium where Kelso had worked. His wife was absent which meant that the Emporium hadn't closed for the funeral. That thought saddened Radine since it spoke of a lack of regard for the dead man.

Radine heard someone enter the church just as Pastor Smith stood to begin the service. Sammy looked back, grinned and slid over to the end of the bench. She glanced over and saw Micah. Her heart took wing as she met his gaze. His brown eyes pled for a truce and her soul filled with pure joy. Radine was so delighted that it was a struggle to keep from grinning right there at the funeral service.

Pastor Smith managed one of his usual ringing orations, and Radine hoped that somewhere in heaven Kelso could hear.

When the last hymn had been sung and the congregation had filed outside, Micah took her elbow and drew her aside. "I'm sorry," he whispered. "I'm truly sorry. You are the finest of ladies and you always make me proud." His eyes spoke of deep regret. "I did act like a jackass—a miserable, jealous, Iowa jackass."

Radine smiled through a film of tears. "I've missed you real bad," she whispered back. "I love you so much."

Neither of the two noticed a gleeful Sammy, grinning from ear to ear in the wagon while Zachariah, Cook and Charity waited with him in the carriage.

Rattling harnesses brought Radine back to reality. "Oh, my," she said. "Everyone seems to be looking at us."

"Let them look." He traced his finger down her cheek. "I'm sorry that it's too late for me to apologize to Nick Kelso for the way I acted but the poor fellow is gone forever."

A cool breeze came from nowhere and chilled Radine. She shivered.

Chapter Five
The Plot Thickens

On Monday Kelso's ghost showed up talking a blue streak. Not out loud like a real person, but silently inside Radine's head. Her mind even heard the teasing lilt of his voice—but without sound.

Pa always claimed she was fey—a person who sometimes connected with the unseen. He had warned her that this ability was both a gift and a responsibility.

The first time Kelso appeared it was early morning and Radine had just finished her sponge-bath. After slipping into an old dress of Mama's, now used for everyday, she brushed her long, naturally curly hair with quick, impatient strokes, pulled it tightly away from her scalp and twisted the unruly tresses into her usual bun. Her curly red hair struggled against any attempt toward order. This mop is harder to control than my temper, she mused.

You don't want to do that, little sister, Kelso spoke inside her head. *Loosen up your tight little fist a bit and fluff that pretty silk around your face. Micah will appreciate the change.*

Too surprised to wonder why Kelso was still earth-bound, she snapped back at him as if he were standing beside her. She spoke back in the same way, silently and inside her head. It seemed to her as if they were conversing normally, even though there was no sound.

"How would you know what Micah likes? You don't know one thing about Micah!"

I know plenty about Micah since I crossed the veil, Kelso said. *I know that he's a good man and I know for sure that he would like to see your pretty hair framing your face. Course I'd have known that anyway. Any man seeing that tight knot of hair on the back of your head would just naturally want to put his fingers into it and pull the whole thing loose.*

"Nick Kelso! How dare you say such a thing to me?" Then a horrible thought entered Radine's mind. "Did you watch me wash and dress?" Heat rose in her cheeks from embarrassment and anger.

'A course not. Such indecencies aren't allowed on this side. I wouldn't have done such a thing anyway. It would have been ungentlemanly.

Radine rolled her eyes and hoped to goodness he was telling the truth. Then she looked critically at herself in the mirror. She had begun wearing a severe hair style when she first came to Guthrie. She'd thought a plain hairstyle would protect her from the unwanted advances of men. She had been alone and unprotected back then, but now with Harriet and the Garrett brothers as friends there would be no need, she realized. She loosened her hair and waves formed naturally.

"Oh, it does look nicer," she said. She remembered a style Harriet sometimes wore and used hair pins to create a French twist. "Yes! I think Micah will like that."

I guarantee it. If you pull loose a tendril on each side by your ears, and cut them so they curl, Micah wouldn't be able to take his eyes off of you. I saw ladies do that in New Orleans and it looked real nice.

"Cut my hair?" Radine said aloud, shocking herself with real sound.

But Kelso was gone.

Kelso's appearance inside her head so unnerved Radine that she kept making silly mistakes. Whatever would Micah say if she accidentally mentioned Kelso's ghost? This worry caused her to miss dusting a lamp table in the lobby and to check Charity's work with an indifferent eye. Even though some of the beds seemed less than perfect, Radine decided the rooms were good enough.

She was eager to get to the pig pen by ten o'clock sharp to meet Micah. Yesterday a railroad car full of lumber needed to be unloaded at the yard. Even on the Sabbath both he and Zachariah worked through the afternoon and until late that night. Would Micah like the way she had changed her hair?

Should she cut curls on each side of her face as Kelso had suggested?

The thought made her heart skip a beat. She ran to her bedroom, grabbed the scissors from her sewing basket and stepped to the small mirror. With a pounding heart she loosened a small hank of hair close to her left ear and stood with scissors in hand gazing at her own image.

How short should she cut it? What if she looked awful? Her hand trembled and she bit her lip. Kelso was a feisty one—could he be teasing her just to make mischief?

The clock in the lobby chimed ten and a cold sweat beaded on her forehead. *I'll miss Micah!* She took a deep breath and snipped. The red strand hung limply. In desperation she used water from her pitcher to wet the hair so she might hide it behind her ear, and then, like a miracle, a curl formed just as Kelso had promised.

"Thank goodness!" Radine said and cut the other side to match. Then she whipped off her apron, ran to the kitchen to grab Esther's morning scraps and headed out the back door. Micah hadn't yet arrived.

A small fission of disappointment flashed through her. Micah was usually early. She worried about how he'd like her hair. Esther grunted anxiously, either begging for her food or sympathizing with Radine.

"I sure hope nothing delays that man, Esther." She threw the scraps into the hog trough just inside the pen. "Some days are enough to make me want to trade places with you, beings as you're safe from anyone's breakfast platter. Folks are not near as sensible as pigs." She took a stick and scratched Esther's head and backbone. Esther grunted with pleasure. "I wish it weren't unladylike to send a note and tell him to hurry because I have a surprise to show him."

Send the note!

Radine blinked and dropped the stick. She looked suspiciously at Esther who moved to finish her last potato peel.

"If you start talking to me I'm moving to Texas!" But she knew the thought had come from her ghost and not from Esther.

To send such a note would be a brazen step. Radine had never in her life pursued a man. She had never needed to. Being born beautiful had its problems, but needing to chase a man hadn't been one of them. She thought back to when

Harriet had asked Zachariah to marry her, and how well their marriage had turned out.

"Well Esther, I reckon there's a time when a woman just has to take control of her own life."

She stepped inside and penned a note, then paid a boy a penny to deliver it. Even if Sammy were around somewhere, he would ask too many questions that she'd rather avoid.

As soon as the boy raced away Radine worried that she had made a mistake and longed to have the note back, but it was too late. She studied her new hair style in the mirror and wondered again if Micah would like the change? Suddenly an appalling thought struck: would Micah think the message she had sent was unladylike? Why on earth had she done such a thing?

Radine longed to tie on her apron and get back to work. Anything but face Micah. She spent a miserable five minutes berating herself then walked back outside to commiserate with Esther.

"Oh Esther," she whispered to the pet. "I've done such a foolish thing!"

Look, Kelso said inside her head. *Look down the alley.*

What she saw shocked her to the soles of her feet. Micah, hatless and with his dark hair flying in the morning breeze, raced toward her in his shirtsleeves. And he was laughing! Not even in Guthrie's early days, when Micah and Zachariah were penniless, had she seen him in public without hat or coat. Such a thing just wasn't done.

In an instant he was lifting her into the air and swinging her around. She laughed with him, dizzy with happiness. Then he set her gently on her feet and kissed the tip of her nose.

"Micah! What if someone sees?"

"Let them. Let all of Guthrie watch."

Everything was perfect. She'd remember this day forever; the wind in Micah's hair, the feel of sunshine on her face, and the two of them standing together, laughing for no reason at all.

"I feared you'd be upset with my note."

"Upset? I was so glad to read it I gave that boy a nickel. There was a mix up with the bill of lading for the new lumber and Zachariah insisted I stay until I figured it out. I was scared to death you'd think I'd forgotten." He paused long enough to kiss her gently on the lips. "When I read that note I didn't care if the whole business went bankrupt. I just ran." He held her at arms length. "You sure look a picture."

"I changed my hair and wanted you to see. Do you like it?"

Micah wrapped one of her side curls around his index finger. "I thought that nothing on earth could make you look more beautiful, but I was wrong. Your hair frames your face like a fiery halo. You take my breath away."

"Oh, Micah."

"Hey, you lovebirds!" Sammy's happy voice shouted from the end of the alley and reminded the couple of where they were. Each took a guilty step away from the other. "Zachariah said to tell Micah that the two of you can spoon later. He said that now he needs you to tend to business."

"Tell my brother I'm tending to the most important business first," Micah said with a laugh. He looked down into Radine's eyes and smiled then he kissed her full on the lips in broad daylight.

Dizzy from the kiss, Radine felt a blush go to her toes but she couldn't stop grinning.

"I'll see you tonight," Micah whispered before turning to walk back to work.

Radine held out her arms and whirled in circles. When dizzy she fell into a heap beside Esther's pen, still laughing. Not since before Mama's death had she been this happy.

Don't you think you should tell him about me?

Radine stopped laughing and looked down the now empty alley. She was so aggravated with Kelso for interrupting her happy dance she spoke aloud.

"Tell Micah? You want me to tell Micah that I'm fey and sit around talking to interfering ghosts? I ought to run out to the cemetery and stomp on your grave."

If that would make you feel better I don't mind a bit.

He was laughing at her! She just knew it! "Why on earth don't you leave me in peace and skedaddle?" Radine snapped.

I wish I could, little missy. I surely do.

Radine had a mental picture of Kelso sitting beside her on the tiny patch of crab grass.

But I can't move on until you figure out who murdered me. As soon as you do that I'll go.

"It seems to me that you're in a better position to know who killed you than I am. You were there!"

I was asleep when someone snuck in, put a pillow over my head, and smothered me. The varmint leaned on me from the back and I couldn't escape.

"And just how am I supposed to solve this murder?"

Guess you'll have to ask a lot of questions and do a lot of deducing. That's the right word, ain't *it?* A cocky lilt to his southern voice rang clearly, even with no sound.

"Isn't it!" Radine corrected. "If you're going to plague me for all eternity, then the least you can do is learn that 'ain't' isn't a proper word."

Chapter Six
A Sleuthing I Will Go

Radine finished her essential morning work quickly. Ignoring more minor chores, she went to her bedroom and took a brand new pink hatbox off the top of her wardrobe. Sighing with pleasure she perused the most elegant hat she had ever seen. She'd bought this extravagance to celebrate her 18th birthday and hadn't shown it to anyone except Cook, and that had been by accident because he saw her carry the hatbox in. She had sworn the Frenchman to silence and hadn't shown anyone else. Not even Micah.

During her years of poverty on the untamed prairie she had always made do. Her bonnets came from picked-out clothes, too threadbare to be mended. She had ripped seams with care and used the odd-shaped pieces to create her own bonnets and dresses.

Radine rode into Guthrie wearing such a dress. The sleeves had come from the backs of Pa's old shirts, the waist from Mama's old everyday dress, the one with an iron burn in front. No piece was large enough for a skirt, so she'd sewn a five yard length of patchwork squares, saved from rags and other scraps of fabric. This had served as her everyday dress. Her best dress was an old gray calico of Ma's, cut down to fit her. The two dresses had been her entire wardrobe.

She had always held her head high, even dressed in these peculiar creations. But in her heart-of-hearts she had always longed for a real store-bought hat. With great pride she set the hat at a saucy angle and smiled at her reflection. Cook had called the lovely concoction her *chapeau* and the French word fit perfectly.

The hat had been chosen with great care. The upper brim and large crown were covered with plaited yellow allover lace and were shirred and ruffled at the edges. A row of white daisies, intertwined with yellow taffeta ribbon, circled the crown and then massed high on one side. She felt truly elegant and wished that Micah could see her now.

Radine told herself she would "save" the hat but that wasn't the real reason. From habit she had always endeavored to keep in the background and never draw attention to herself. When she finally decided to wear the hat every eye would turn toward her. At least she hoped that was what would happen. She carefully put her treasure back in the box and donned her old bonnet.

First she walked to the Emporium to speak with Kelso's former employer. It seemed impossible that anyone at the funeral had murdered Kelso—every person attending had been a well-known Guthrie citizen. But both her intuition and her common sense told her the culprit had to be someone in this group.

A "Help Wanted" sign sat in the window and a bell fastened to the door tinkled as she entered. After the usual greetings, she gave the owner her list.

"You have any applicants for Mr. Kelso's job yet?" she asked as an opening to the other questions she really wanted to ask.

"No one I can use." The merchant adjusted his wire-rimmed glasses and studied the list. "The job requires someone who can not only read, write and cipher, but also who is strong enough to load 100 pound sacks of flour and other heavy things into customer's wagons. There are plenty of strong backs, but no one with the book learning."

Kelso was educated? She should have been surprised, but wasn't. Many drifters had good education. You just never could tell. And it made her happy to know that Kelso had enjoyed the pleasure of reading during his short life.

"Mr. Kelso knew how to read and write, did he?"

"Sure could. I guess there's some good to being raised in an orphanage." The man began assembling items from Radine's list.

"He was an orphan?" A wave of sympathy washed through her. That was something that she and Kelso had in common.

"Yep, and he was the best help I ever had. In fact, he was *too* good. Both Mr. Hightower and Mr. Bingham offered him jobs, and he was a fixin' to leave me."

"Both of them? That seems mighty strange." Radine frowned. Jobs were scarce in Guthrie just then and it seemed unlikely that two such important citizens would want to hire the same man.

"You wouldn't have thought so if you'd seen him work with numbers. He could scan a column of figures and then almost immediately write the sum at the bottom." The owner licked his pencil and crossed off an item on Radine's list.

"He could? Are you sure?" Radine was quick with numbers, but she couldn't add that fast.

"Surprised me too. First time I saw him do that I was furious. I thought he'd lied about being able to add and subtract and was just making up a sum. I totaled the ticket myself and dad blamed if he didn't have the right answer."

"I never heard of such a thing."

"Me neither. Hightower noticed it right away and asked him to come over to the bank for a chat. I knew then and there that I'd lose him. Then Mr. Bingham from the railroad office came in, took one look at Kelso and wanted to hire him, too." He wrote something on the hotel's store tab, taking time to carefully add the figures.

"So, who was he going to work for?"

"The bank. He gave me a month's notice the same day that Slick O'Reilly stabbed him."

Radine figured this was why the man hadn't closed the Emporium for the funeral. He probably felt miffed at losing such good help.

"So he was raised in an orphanage? Where 'bouts did Mr. Kelso come from, anyway?" Radine asked.

"From down South somewhere, Beaumont, I think he said but the orphanage where he grew up was in Arkansas."

"You must have learned a lot about him while he worked for you."

"No, can't say that I did." He peered over his glasses at Radine. "As I recollect he asked *me* questions, and mostly about the folks in town. Guess he planned to settle here and wanted to know who was who."

The merchant put the last item in a box and smiled. "I put this on the hotel tab for you. Is Sammy going to come by and pick it up later on?"

"Yes, he'll be by as usual to carry it to the hotel."

The bell over the door rang and a farmer wearing a white shirt with his overalls walked into the store. It was Radine's cue to say goodbye and leave. She crossed the street and walked down one block to the bank where she asked to speak to Mr. Hightower privately. The two had met for the first time about a year before. The circumstances were unhappy, but each had formed a sort of grudging respect for the other. She figured that was why the banker came to her birthday party and brought a gift.

She studied the tall, somber man before her: a shrewd businessman, homely yet dignified. The only way to get any answers would be with total honesty. She spoke quickly and without pausing so he couldn't interrupt before she'd said her piece.

"Mr. Hightower, I know that you were going to hire Nick Kelso to work in the bank and you must know that he died in my bed. What you couldn't know is that for personal reasons I feel a powerful responsibility to find out who killed him."

He listened without any hint of interrupting, so Radine risked taking a much needed breath. "I thought maybe he has folks somewhere who'd like to know of his passing." That was all of the truth she dared to share. She glanced down at what seemed like chicken tracks on the ink blotter that covered the desk, then back up to meet his gaze.

A muscle in Hightower's jaw twitched, as if he were fighting a smile but that was his only change of expression. Radine felt a glimmer of hope and pressed on.

"You'll have to take my word that this isn't just idle curiosity on my part. I figure that since you showed up at Kelso's funeral you must really have liked him."

Hightower's eyes saddened, he leaned back in his chair and built a steeple with his fingers. "Yes, I did. Very much. He was brilliant with numbers, got along well with people, and was ambitious to better himself. He'd just discovered love and planned on settling down and making Guthrie his home." A look of remembered pain showed in the banker's eyes and then was quickly hidden. "The death of anyone so young is a great tragedy."

"Then you knew he was in love with Cinda Smith?"

"Yes. He told me he wanted to marry her, and that was another reason I wanted to hire him. People feel safer when their money is in the hands of a family man."

"How did her Ma and Pa feel about the match? I'll bet that when Kelso's prospects improved they got a lot happier for him to come courting?"

It was a minute before Hightower answered. He stood and walked to the window. "Does that really matter now?"

"It might." Had he turned his back to hide his feelings? She frowned and pressed on. "Did the Smith's have something against Kelso?"

Hightower faced her and sighed. "These are private matters that concern patrons of mine. I really can't discuss personal information." He sat back down in his chair. "I had hoped that giving the young man a permanent job in my bank would make him an acceptable son-in-law. I planned on training him to be an accountant." He shook his head. "It didn't seem to help much."

"But an accountant is a real respectable job. Nothing wrong with a preacher's daughter marrying a bank accountant." Or a store clerk either, in Radine's opinion, but she didn't say so.

"I couldn't understand it either," Hightower said.

Radine glanced toward the brass clock on the wall and bit her lip. "I've taken up too much of your time, Mr. Hightower, but I do appreciate your talking to me." She stood and smiled at him, "We're having chicken pie at the café for lunch. That's your favorite, isn't it?"

Hightower studied her. He cocked one bushy eyebrow before answering. "Miss Radine, I've seen that look on your face once before and it worries me to see it again. Please be careful. Remember that you can come to me any time that you need help."

Radine left the bank glowing from the kindness shown to her by the banker, but she wished to goodness that everything she thought didn't show on her face for all the world to read like a primer.

The lumberyard was visible in the distance and Radine hoped to catch at least a glimpse of Micah. If he saw her she knew he'd head her way, but only Zachariah and Sammy were outside serving customers. Micah had to be at his desk working on accounts. Thoughts of her beau quickened her pulse and she smiled. Then she remembered her irksome ghost and bit her lip.

There wasn't a minute to lose. She had to solve this puzzle and get Kelso on his way up to heaven where he was supposed to be. Her next stop was the undertakers. Maybe she could find out who paid for the fancy funeral.

A bell again announced her entrance and after a minute the undertaker stepped into the room.

"Why Miss Morgan," he said. "What an unexpected pleasure. I hope nothing tragic has brought you to my door."

"No, nothing like that," Radine said, gathering her thoughts. She knew the man would be shocked and possibly offended at direct queries. So instead of blurting out a question with her usual bluntness, she pretended to thank him for donating the elegant casket, as if she thought he had furnished the thing himself.

"I'm going to tell everyone in town about your kindness in burying poor Mr. Kelso in such a fine coffin. I think that such generosity should be heralded far and wide but first I thought I should thank you personally."

The man's mouth dropped open in surprise and horror. "But I didn't pay for that casket!"

He didn't mention the name of the donor as she had hoped he might, so she tried again.

"Well then, it must have been Mr. Hightower. I know he was right fond of Mr. Kelso, he told me so himself."

"It wasn't him at all. He offered to pay for a pine box, though. It's astonishing that two of our finest businessmen thought so highly of that boy."

Radine's mind raced. Finest men? It couldn't have been Harriet's Uncle Richard, because he'd been gone for a month on a trip to Kansas City. She mentally reviewed those present at the funeral and there was only two who fit the description. Mortimer Hightower and Luther Bingham!

"Ah, then it was Mr. Bingham. We surely have a lot of good men in this town."

Luther Bingham wasn't one of Radine's favorite people even if he did live at the Grand Hotel but when the funeral director neither agreed nor disagreed, Radine knew she'd struck pay dirt.

Next stop on her list was Doc Johnson's office, but when she stopped by he was stitching up a boy's foot and she decided not to wait. She glanced at the sun to guess the time and decided to head back to the hotel. She'd take Harriet some lunch and then run down to the pigpen for a minute. It seemed an odd thing to do, but when she talked over a problem with that red pig a good solution often came to mind.

Chapter Seven
Two Heads Are Better Than One

Radine carried a lunch tray up to Harriet thinking they would eat together and discuss baby clothes. To her surprise the conversation took an unexpected turn.

"I'm bored to tears with my own company, and God forgive me, I'm even tired of 'baby talk.' What I really want to know is how your sleuthing is coming along." Harriet smiled expectantly.

"Sleuthing? I came to talk about a layette for twins." Radine poured tea a bit more carefully than was necessary. She knew that Zachariah would pitch a fit if Harriet became involved with ghosts and murder. Always protective of his beloved wife, he had developed into a fierce watchdog during her pregnancy. The last thing Radine needed was for this father-to-be to cast grim looks of betrayal in her direction. "I brought a tablet and a pencil so we could make a list of the baby items you'll need."

"Don't try to divert me, Radine Morgan," Harriet said with a laugh. "Do you think I've lost my ability to reason as well as my ability to navigate stairs? Of course you're sleuthing. On Friday Dr. Johnson told me that Mr. Kelso would be fine. Then suddenly he's dead. The good doctor refuses to discuss the subject. I've asked several times and he lapses into a long dissertation about peppermint leaves for indigestion and chamomile tea for insomnia. I know better than ask Zachariah or Micah. When I ask Sammy he looks at me as if he's trapped—like a rabbit facing a coyote. Will you please tell me what's going on?"

Radine met Harriett's gaze. "Doc's just doing his job. It's important to have a quiet stomach and get a good night's sleep. He's just taking good care of you."

"But I don't suffer from either complaint." Harriet leaned back in her chair and raised an eyebrow. "Tell me what's going on before *I* commit both murder and mayhem."

"There's nothing going on that you'd care one whit about." Radine set two plates of chicken pie on a small table to distract her friend with the mouth watering food. Chunks of chicken and vegetables smothered in a rich cream sauce and topped with golden biscuits smelled scrumptious enough to make her mouth water. But Harriett looked unimpressed.

"My brain isn't pregnant! Kelso didn't have enough time to become septic. Doctor Johnson is going about with a haunted expression, so I know something bad happened. Also, you've been wearing your crime-solving face since Saturday."

"My what?"

"Your sleuthing face. The one you wore while threading through the clues to the murder of your friend Ida Mae. You forget that I know you so well, my dear."

Radine threw up her hands in exasperation. "Oh Harriet, what am I going to do with you? I don't want to talk about any of this for fear you'll want to help me solve the crime."

"Well, I do. What's wrong with that?"

"It's too dangerous! You can't go about asking questions in your condition. At best you'll either overdo or fall. But the main thing wrong with the idea is that Zachariah would string my carcass up on the nearest cottonwood if I got you involved in another murder!"

"Pshaw, he'll do no such thing. Besides, expecting a baby or not, I'm a grown woman and I make my own decisions." Harriet at last noticed the chicken and smiled. She took a dainty bite. "Ummm...Cook has outdone himself today. This is wonderful."

"I'm glad to see that you finally remembered that you're eating for three." Radine grinned and attacked her own plate with appetite. They ate in silence for a few minutes and Radine began to hope her friend had forgotten about Kelso. She was about to suggest birdseye instead of flannel for diapers when Harriet paused with her fork midway between plate and mouth.

"You know very well that there's nothing wrong with my brain. I can sit here and think however big I might be. Would you tell me what has happened? I'm dying of boredom and a nice mystery to solve is just what I need to pass the time. Either you tell me what you know or I'm going out on my own this very afternoon and begin asking questions."

"You wouldn't dare," Radine said, knowing very well that when Harriet's dander was up this quiet, refined woman would dare anything.

Harriet didn't argue, she just looked straight at her friend without smiling or speaking.

Radine rolled her eyes. "Of course you would," she said. "If I share everything I know, will you promise to only sit and think and not gad about all over town asking questions? I've always said that you have the finest brain-box in Oklahoma Territory."

"I promise," Harriet said.

So the two friends finished lunch, then sipped tea as Radine told her friend everything that had happened, including *The Bad Feeling* and the appearance of Kelso's ghost.

"I'm counting on you not to think that my brain is scrambled," Radine said. "I know ghosts and other-world warnings sound queer, but I swear that Kelso's ghost won't leave Grand Hotel until I figure out who murdered him."

"I believe you, dear Radine. Your touch with the Other Side helped us solve our last mystery. I know your mother touches your spirit and warns you when danger is near. It doesn't seem so unlikely that she would also communicate with Mr. Kelso when he needed help."

Relief washed through Radine. It was as if a heavy load shifted from her shoulders. Sharing with Harriet was even better than telling Esther.

"It's real puzzling that Mr. Bingham would pay for Kelso's burial, especially such a fine casket," Radine said. "He just isn't that prone to charity."

"I agree," Harriet said. "When that question is answered, I think we'll have an important key to this puzzle."

"This afternoon I'm going to try and speak to Doc again. I'm hoping he'll shed some light on why Kelso died so suddenly. He knows something that he's not telling, and I wonder if it might have to do with Kelso and Cinda's romance?"

"That's possible. After I gave up hope of getting the answers I wanted, the doctor and I had one of our usual philosophical conversations, discussing life and people in general. As he left Doctor Johnson asked me the strangest question."

"He did? What was it?"

"Would a person ever be justified in sacrificing a villain who has often escaped justice, to protect a guilty person who is basically good?"

Radine gasped. "He knows who killed Kelso!"

Chapter Eight
Another Suspect

Radine left Harriet to her afternoon nap and walked down the second floor corridor carrying the tray filled with dirty dishes. A bedroom door swung open and Charity's plump backside almost knocked the tray out of her hands.

"Watch where you're going," Radine said.

Charity let out a tiny shriek and whirled around, then smiled at her boss. "Miss Radine, you scared me out of 10 years of growth. I was checking to make double sure that Mr. Bingham's room was spotless."

"Mr. Bingham's room should have been cleaned this morning. What if he had come upstairs at lunchtime and found his bed unmade?"

"Oh, I was in earlier to empty slops, make the bed and red up but I noticed he stopped by his room after lunch. I decided to spiff everything up again."

Radine frowned and the chambermaid's face reddened.

"And why does Mr. Bingham get all of this extra service?" Radine asked. If a guest was taking advantage of Charity's youth, she meant to put a stop to any improper behavior. She didn't care how rich or important the man might be. After all, the girl was a whole year younger than she.

"He tipped me a quarter last week!" Charity's eyes grew round and she lowered her voice to almost a whisper. "He never did such a thing before and I want to keep him in a good mood."

"A quarter? No wonder you're smiling." Suspicion prickled down Radine's spine. "When did this happen?"

"It was Friday and he came downstairs especially to find me and tip me. Said he appreciated how I kept his room so nice and tidy."

For a minute it was hard to breathe. "Friday? What time Friday?" No guest ever walked down to the service area to tip a maid. Back when she was cleaning the rooms a businessman from Chicago had once left three pennies on his washstand but most folks traveling through Guthrie didn't tip chambermaids.

"Well, let me see." Charity leaned against her dust mop and thought for a minute. I was just emptying my last chamber pot so it must have been about ten thirty or so." She giggled. "At first I thought he might be looking for the gent's room 'cause he looked upset when he saw me. His face even turned red. Then he reached into his pocket for the quarter. 'For your good service,' he said."

Radine blinked. Bingham tipped Charity a quarter? Paid to bury Kelso in an expensive coffin? Why?

"Who else did you see in the service area that morning?"

"Well, there was Cook, and Sammy, and the farmer delivering fresh eggs, and..."

"Not folks with a reason to be there," Radine said. "Did anyone come into the hall or kitchen who you didn't expect to see there?"

Charity cocked her head to one side and thought for a minute. "No, everyone else comes regularly."

Radine continued her way down the stairs and into the kitchen with her mind racing.

On the day Nick Kelso died, Luther Bingham was close by. His presence looked suspicious, but why on earth would he murder a store clerk? And after he had offered him a job?

Kelso was just one of many men who came to Oklahoma Territory to seek his fortune. It looked as if he had been doing well when suddenly his life was over. Erased like a misspelled word on a slate board.

Luther Bingham was now her number one suspect. Not for one minute did she believe that he came downstairs to give Charity a quarter. That was nothing but a bold-faced lie to explain why he was where he oughtn't to be but she didn't want to close her mind to other possibilities.

Radine left the tray in the kitchen, and stepped into her small apartment to find her tablet and pencil. Someone could have slipped inside through the alley and into her rooms. She had cried into her apron for quite a spell and wouldn't have noticed even if a big yellow dog had walked in. Maybe Esther had seen someone, but she wasn't talking.

Harriet had planned the location of Radine's rooms. She'd wanted her friend to be able to come and go without being observed by nosy townsfolk. For the first time Radine saw a drawback to her formerly valued privacy.

She settled herself at her small desk and wrote the name *Luther Bingham*. She'd also write down the names of anyone, however unlikely, who had been near enough to slip into the hotel and kill Kelso.

Radine chewed her pencil for a minute and frowned. She didn't want to write the next name, but experience had taught her that the most unexpected folk sometimes committed murder. Everyone, she had found, had a secret from their past, and some were willing to kill to protect that secret.

She sighed and penned the name *Emmaline Smith*. Then to be fair she listed *Doc Johnson, Cook* and *Charity*. The last entries seemed absurd and she smiled. What would these three think if they learned their names were on her murder suspect list?

The clock chimed thrice and Radine jumped to her feet. Where had the time gone? She put away her tablet and walked over to the supply inventory she had worked on yesterday.

Radine had just finished inspecting and counting the last of the hotel linen when the clock chimed five. She intended to deliver the prisoner's supper herself instead of sending Sammy as she usually did. It would provide an opportunity for her to quiz both the deputy and the card sharp.

When she picked up the jailhouse tray, Cook offered to go instead, insisting she had no business being in the company of criminals. Radine was flattered that Cook would think her too refined to step inside a jail. However, she had no intention of losing a chance to sleuth.

"Don't fret about me, Cook, I was raised on the prairie and I can take care of myself." She picked up the napkin-covered tray and doubled-stepped out of the kitchen before he could argue.

Deputy Daniels spied her walking past his window. When she reached the door he opened it before she could knock. He took the tray and said the U.S. Marshall would take O'Reilly to Ft. Smith on Thursday to face Hanging Judge Parker and there would be no need for food after that. She followed him through the office to a cell in back. The prisoner, haggard and sullen looking, eyed Radine. Deputy Daniels instructed his prisoner to step to the back of the cell. He then unlocked the door with a large black key, set the food on the floor then re-locked the cell.

"I'd like to ask Mr. O'Reilly a few questions," she said.

"No, ma'am, I don't think so," Daniels answered.

"I'll stand way back here where I'll be safe." Radine smiled sweetly in the hopes of changing his mind.

The deputy opened his mouth to protest, and then closed it again. He stood silent for a minute. Radine figured he was remembering her last run-in with murder and her determination to do as she pleased.

"I guess there's no chance of reasoning with you. You can speak to him, but I'll be right in the next room if he gets disrespectful." He turned to the prisoner. "You mind your manners with this young lady." Then he spoke to Radine in an undertone. "You have five minutes, Miss Morgan."

Radine would have preferred to have spoken to Slick without anyone close enough to listen, but she couldn't ask the Deputy to leave his own jail.

She glanced at Slick who had already wolfed down half of his meal. He seemed to sense her attention and paused for a second to switch his gaze to her. His eyes swept down her body with insulting insolence. Heat rose unbidden to her cheeks. She felt angry and violated, but she was helpless as to how to dress him down without exposing herself to worse insult. She longed for Harriet's presence. Her friend was such a fine lady that even this cad wouldn't have dared such impertinence.

"You're a fine looking woman, Radine Morgan," Slick said with a leer.

Furious that he knew her name, Radine stared back coolly. She held her head high and gave him her best rendition of a cold look, just as she had seen Harriet do when some man in from the trail was too bold.

"I'm here to talk to you about the night you stabbed Nick Kelso."

"Bah! I've been wrongly accused of murdering that greenhorn. All I did was give him a little scratch with my

Bowie knife, and a real man wouldn't even have taken notice."

"I don't think you killed him." *Even though you are a low-down snake in the grass,* she wanted to add, but didn't. "I intend to find out who did."

Slick's mouth fell open with surprise then he snorted in mockery. "You? Why would you believe me? Anyway, what could a woman do?"

"If you don't want help then I'm leaving. When the deputy hauls you to Ft. Smith and Judge Parker stretches your neck, it'll serve you right." Radine whirled on her heel and headed toward the door.

"Wait," Slick said. "I didn't mean nothin' by what I said."

"Yes you did. And if you don't want to hang you'll tell me the truth about what happened Friday night when you stabbed Kelso."

The truth came hard to the card sharp, but Radine quizzed him until she learned everything he knew. The truth wasn't pretty, but it wasn't murder, either. Nick Kelso had been lucky at cards, and being smart, he'd stepped away while he was ahead. Slick wasn't used to this kind of wisdom and he had wanted his money back. He caught up with Kelso in the dark and stabbed and robbed him. Then he hightailed it out of town with the cash. Deputy Daniels overtook him on the trail and arrested him.

"I made sure the wound wasn't fatal. I know how to hurt a man bad without killing him. This is Guthrie, and City Deputy Daniels isn't a man to reckon with. I knew he'd come after me, but wouldn't follow me too far if I didn't kill the boy. It was my bad luck that Daniels had a faster horse than me."

Radine walked away musing over what the gambler had said and suddenly Kelso was there. His voice rang inside her head, clear as a bell and he was madder than a wet rooster.

I wanted to clean that lowdown slimy coyote's plow and a few days ago I'd have done just that. I swung at him in that jail until my arms ached, and he didn't even know I was there. Sometimes being a ghost is downright inconvenient!

"I didn't know you were there," Radine said. "You need to let me know when you're around. I like to know what's going on."

You wouldn't listen. But I know what you need to do next. You need to walk right over to the lumberyard and demand that Micah bloody that varmint's nose. Why if that man of yours heard what I heard, he'd be mad enough to chew penny nails and spit them out like bullets.

"I don't need you giving me advice. Micah's just now over being jealous about you. If he finds out you are still hanging around, he'll be furious again."

But I'm dead!

"And that's supposed to make it better? You want me to tell him a ghost has asked me to solve his murder? Why he'd think I was insane."

That man's so crazy in love with you, he'd want to marry you even if you were *loony. You couldn't drive him away with a pitchfork.*

Radine grinned. It sure was hard to be mad at Kelso when he said something like that to her. A glow of happiness spread through her, but she felt impelled to argue.

"How would you know what Micah feels?"

I know because I'm on this side of the veil and I know a lot of things I didn't know before. But I don't know who killed me and that's why I need you to go around and talk to folks. It's past time for me to be gone but I'm not leaving until I know the truth.

"If you're not the most troublesome creature who ever died!" Radine snapped. "Because of you I'm walking on eggshells whenever I talk to Micah, afraid I'll let something slip that should be kept quiet."

He's a sensible man. Just explain to him what's happened. He'll understand.

"And let him think I'm touched? That I talk to ghosts? For sure he'd never marry me then. Who wants a crazy wife?"

Then I guess the only thing you can do is to solve my murder, Kelso said, and Radine imagined she heard his silent laugh. *Because I'm not leaving until you do.*

Chapter Nine
Doc Shares a Secret

After sleeping on the problem, Radine decided to come right out and ask Doc Johnson who had killed Kelso. Not that he would tell her. She figured he hadn't even told Deputy Daniels but if she could get the old man to reminisce, he might slip up and tell some tiny fact that would help piece the puzzle together.

Micah showed up at the hotel café at six-thirty for his usual breakfast before opening the lumberyard. His face lighted like a Christmas tree when she slipped through the kitchen door and sat opposite him at his usual table for two.

She carried in her usual breakfast, a bowl of oatmeal sprinkled with raisins, as well as a plate piled high with bacon, eggs and biscuits for Micah. With her plans for the day she had to make every minute count and nothing was as important to her as Micah.

Radine poured coffee for them both and they ate in a happy silence, their eyes doing most of the talking. Their smiles told the rest of Guthrie that all was well with the couple. Sammy swung in and out the kitchen door busing the tables in the busy café. He stole glances at the pair, but he didn't say a word. His smile lighted the whole room. If Kelso was around, the ghost wasn't talking.

Just after Micah left for the lumberyard, she saw Doc Johnson drive his buggy past the hotel toward the stable. With one hand she untied her apron and with the other snagged a basket so she could take him a hot breakfast. Doc looked exhausted and she figured he'd been out all night delivering a baby. She ran to the kitchen and grabbed a couple of hot biscuits and stuffed them with fried eggs and sausage patties being kept warm on the large stove. If Cook meant the food to be for his own breakfast he'd just have to forgive her.

Forgetting her resolution to always act like a lady, she ran to the stable and caught Doc as he walked away, his medical bag in hand.

"Does Mrs. Garrett need help?" Doc said when he saw Radine.

"No, she's fine. I saw you ride into town looking like the cats dragged you in, so I took it on myself to bring you breakfast. I'll walk with you to your office and make you some coffee."

"Mighty kind of you, Miss Radine," Doc said. "I'm much obliged, but I should warn you that I'm too tired to talk about how Nick Kelso died just now."

Radine opened her mouth to deny the accusation, then laughed instead. "Guess you know me pretty well," she said. "But you're going to need this here breakfast anyway. That means that while you're eating you'll have to put up with me." Radine grinned. "And I warn you that I'm a woman who likes to talk."

Doc chuckled. "You do beat all, Miss Radine." He stepped up to the porch of his office and fished a key from his pocket. "Come in, I'll be glad of your company while I have a bite to eat." He held the door for Radine and they walked through to a larger room in the back that he used primarily for seeing patients.

"I'm closing this connecting door, too, so I can eat in peace. Folks know to call out whenever they come in if they have something that can't wait."

Radine struck a match to the kindling already laid in the small box stove, then slowly added coal. Used in the winter for heat, the stove also served for boiling water to sterilize instruments and to make coffee. She dipped water from a bucket into a blackened granite pot, measured in a generous amount of coffee, and set it on the already hot stove.

Doc collapsed in a chair beside his roll top desk and massaged his temples. Radine figured he was going to talk about the baby he had just delivered. She didn't have time for idle chatter, so she spoke first.

"Nick Kelso didn't die from that gambler's stab wound, did he?" she asked in her usual blunt manner.

Doc blinked in surprise, then shook his head. "Couldn't have, but I hope you won't spread that information around town."

"I ain't no gossip," Radine said, once again forgetting proper grammar. "But I think it's wrong for an innocent man to die on the gallows even if he is a crooked card sharp and no telling what else."

Doc studied her with his bloodshot eyes. "Maybe he didn't kill Kelso, but he's not innocent. I know for sure he murdered a helpless old man, but the crime couldn't be proved so he went scot-free." Doc pulled the napkin-covered meal from the basket and attacked it with enthusiasm without waiting for coffee.

Radine glanced at the color of the brew now bubbling in the glass dome of the pot, decided it was ready to pour and filled Doc's cup.

"I've got to find out who killed Kelso," she said. "If you won't tell me I'll learn somewhere else."

"Why have you decided that you're Mistress Sherlock Holmes? It makes me mighty uneasy for you to mess around with murder."

Radine smiled. "I'll admit that I love reading a tale with a good puzzle, but Mr. Holmes isn't the reason I have to know about Kelso."

Doc sipped his coffee and ruminated. "Does this need-to-know have anything to do with that argument between you and Micah?"

Radine felt color rise in her cheeks, and she studied the tips of her neatly trimmed fingernails. "Sammy's got a big mouth," she said.

"The boy is worried and he knew that I wouldn't tell anyone."

"We've made up," she said. "Micah isn't mad at me anymore."

"Glad to hear that. It's a hard thing to be jealous of a dead man but I don't understand how finding Kelso's murderer would help?" He took another big bite of the biscuit and sausage sandwich and chewed for a minute. "Unless, of course, his ghost is prowling around and pestering the daylights out of you?"

Radine's mouth dropped open in shock. "Why on earth would you say such a thing?"

"I'm an old man and I've observed human nature for a long time. Now and again I've come across a person who seems to have second-sight." He took a deep swig of coffee and sighed. "And you, Miss Radine, are such a person."

"I don't want to be." She felt suddenly limp and stared helplessly at the old man.

"I know," Doc said. "Those with a gift of this sort never want to have it. It's a heavy burden. You see and know things that most folk don't have to worry about."

The two sat in silence while Doc finished his meal. Then he wiped his fingers and mouth on the linen napkin and reached to take her hand.

"Because of that I'm going to help you if I can. Even though I think it's a dangerous path for you to tread upon. You must promise me to be careful."

Radine knew what he said was true. She and Harriet had come close to being trapped by a murderer just last year when they investigated the death of the saloon girl, Ida Mae Hawkins. She also wondered why she hadn't sensed her dear Mama's presence in the last few days. It was almost as if Mama was sending Kelso instead.

"I'll be careful," she promised.

Doc held up his cup for a refill, sipped the hot coffee and frowned into the distance.

"As you've already guessed, Kelso didn't die from the stab wound." He stared into space for a minute and sighed.

Radine bit her lip to keep from urging him to get on with the story and to be quick about it. Such impudence would not only be disrespectful, her impatience also might irk the old man and turn him stubborn. The good doctor would take his own sweet time. By the time he answered, she could taste her own blood.

"In a way it is Slick's fault that Kelso died, but we both know that he couldn't be the one who slipped into your room and smothered that poor man with a pillow."

"With my pillow? In my bed?" The same pillow she had slept so soundly on last night? She shuddered. Tonight she must slip a table knife between the facing and the door to keep out the villains.

"Someone evidently was watching and when you stepped out that person came in. He or she caught Kelso napping and held a pillow over his face."

Easy and quick and not even messy, Radine thought. She studied the doctor for a minute. "You haven't told this to the deputy, have you?"

Doc remained silent for a long time before he spoke. "No, and I'm not going to. I know for sure that Slick O'Reilly killed that fellow in Oklahoma City, and just because there's no proof doesn't mean he shouldn't hang."

Radine's quick mind analyzed what Doc *hadn't* said as well as what he had said.

"You know who killed him, don't you?"

Doc opened his mouth and then closed it again. "You're the beatenest female I ever knew. Micah Garrett is in for a challenging life when he teams up with a woman who knows what he's thinking before the words come out of his mouth."

"Tell me who it was, Doc. I have to know."

Doc paused again and Radine was sure he was going to turn her down. Finally he shook his head and threw up his hands in defeat.

"I don't know for sure but I can tell you young Kelso's sad history if you promise not to tell anyone else."

It was Radine's turn to think before answering. She loved justice, but her main objective was to send Kelso on his way. She frowned, recalling the ghost's exact words and remembered that he'd promised to leave after she told him who killed him.

"I promise," she said. "I won't tell a *living* soul." This was a promise she could keep.

Doc wearily closed his eyes for a minute, shook his head then began speaking.

"Life isn't black and white," he said. "It's a series of different shades of gray and faded blues and sad lavenders along with some black and some white."

Radine blinked, surprised that Doc had waxed poetic all of a sudden. Who on earth had killed Kelso, she wondered? But she held her tongue and gazed expectantly at the old man.

"Like I said, he was smothered," he said with a sigh.

"Why didn't Kelso yell for help?"

"I figure he was sleeping when the attack occurred. It wouldn't take a lot of strength to quietly walk in, slip the pillow from under his head and hold it over his face. If he were sleeping soundly, by the time he realized what was happening it would have been too late."

"That was cold-blooded murder! The slaughter of an innocent man! How could you not tell the deputy? How could you make me promise to not tell?" Outrage swelled inside Radine's chest. "You tricked me into silence! How could you?"

Doc held up one hand as if to fend off an attack. "You haven't heard the whole story. When you do, I think you'll understand, at least I hope you will."

Radine nodded curtly, but she didn't think she could ever understand smothering a sleeping man. What could be more dastardly or cowardly? She bit her tongue, crossed her arms and stared at the good doctor.

"Remember that you've given me your word never to tell one living soul," Doc said.

"I remember, but I'm not promising you another thing, ever." Radine scowled.

"I understand your anger, and I'll trust you even if you don't trust me." Doc made a steeple of his fingers, closed his eyes and began telling a story that obviously distressed him very much.

Chapter Ten
A Tragic Story and an Odd Coincidence

"Life is mighty strange sometimes." Doc Johnson stared into his half-empty coffee cup as if he might find an answer to life's tragedies somewhere in the black brew. "About twenty-five years ago I was practicing medicine in a prosperous town in southern Missouri and a young man and a young woman fell in love. Her father was the minister of a large local church and a very important man. The young fellow came from a poor family and he had no prospects at the time, so the girl's parents opposed the match." He paused to take another sip.

"But love isn't always wise and the couple gave in to temptation. Hoping to set things right, the young man asked for the hand of his beloved, but the girl's father refused his permission. Determined to prove his worth, the young man accepted a job from one of the railroads and set off to make his fortune."

The story caught at Radine's heart and she knew the ending would not be a happy one. A father forcing his will on a daughter was a common occurrence, and anger at the unfairness caused her to sit very straight. Doc harrumphed and continued speaking.

"After the man had been gone for a month, the young woman realized she was expecting a child and she became panic stricken. She wrote to her young man at once, begging him to come home and rescue her."

"But he didn't?" Radine said.

"No. In desperation she married another man 20 years her senior who was also pursuing her. She naively hoped he would think the child was his."

"But I reckon he could count to nine," Radine said.

"He could. The husband didn't call me to deliver the baby but used a midwife, as many folks did. He chose a woman who was desperate for money and he paid her extra to tell his wife the baby boy was stillborn. The husband sent the baby to an orphanage down in Arkansas. The young mother grieved for her lost child but in another year she gave birth to a little girl."

"That poor woman," Radine said. "Was she the one who told you this awful story?"

"No, it was the midwife as she was dying. She said she had to unburden her soul." Doc paused and cleared his throat. "The midwife was asked to take the baby to the orphanage. Smith gave her a piece of his wife's jewelry in addition to paying her fifty dollars in gold. She left the jewelry for the baby, said doing that made her feel less guilty."

"I don't blame her." Impotent anger flared red hot inside Radine, but she bit her lip and bade her temper to stay calm. She needed to be able to think with a clear mind. "I guess that baby boy was Kelso?"

"He was. Fate must have an evil sense of humor, because not only did the mother, her spouse and her daughter end up in Guthrie, but Kelso's real father also came here too."

"Well, I'd like to give that snake a piece of my mind. Why didn't he go back and marry that poor girl like a decent man?"

"He never received her letter. The girl's father had made a pact with the Postmaster to pass any correspondence from her back to him."

"But that's against the law!"

"Small towns have their own laws. The two men were lifelong friends, and the father was very influential." Doc sighed and drained his cup.

The outside door banged against a wall and noisy footsteps sounded in the outer office. The inner door flew open and a worried-looking woman rushed in with a girl of about eleven. The child's hand was wrapped in a towel and she was crying. Both Doc and Radine jumped to their feet and rushed to help.

"My daughter burned her hand real bad on the flat iron," the woman said. "I'm sure glad you're in your office."

While Doc treated the injury other patients started lining up in the waiting room. Radine knew her questions would have to wait until after office hours. She excused herself and walked back to the hotel mulling over what she had learned.

She longed to discuss her thoughts with Micah or her friend Harriet, but she had given her word to tell no one... no one living, at least.

What did you learn from Doc? Kelso's silent voice asked.

"I wondered when you'd turn up."

You're stalling.

"I'm not. I figured you were in the office eavesdropping like you always do."

"No, I just got here."

"If you want me to solve this murder you're going to have to trust me. Now go away and let me think!"

And to her surprise, Nick Kelso stopped talking.

Radine's brain raced with ideas as she performed her morning tasks. Each young woman in the area who might be the second child was considered. She discarded names one by one until only Cinda Smith remained. Her mother Emmaline tried to be cheerful, but there had always been a sadness in the woman. Then sudden shock stunned Radine. If Cinda was that child, she would be Kelso's *half sister!*

What an unbearable thought! Radine racked her brain searching for another young woman who might fit the facts, but an inner knowing whispered to Radine that her guess was right. None of the others fit the description so perfectly. Cinda had a mother whose husband was much older, both parents were educated, and she knew for sure that family had come from southern Missouri.

A sickness of heart washed through Radine. Did Kelso know? And if so, did he learn before he was murdered? That seemed unlikely to her, he'd been too happy about being in love and he had spoken of matrimony with Cinda.

His murder may have prevented an unthinkable marriage, but why not just tell Kelso the truth and ask him to leave town? He didn't seem the sort of man to tell a sordid story that would ruin the reputation of the girl he loved. Not even to revenge himself. But of course there would be no way for the murderer to know that.

The story she had heard from Doc provided a strong motive for Emmaline, Luther Bingham or Pastor Smith. None of these would want this scandal to be made public. Each had too much to lose. Pastor Smith couldn't be the murderer, though because he hadn't been near her room that morning. Neither Charity nor Cook had mentioned him as an unexpected visitor when she asked. That left Luther Bingham and Emmaline Smith.

Even though Luther Bingham was Kelso's father, it was hard for Radine to imagine the pompous businessman as a young man in love. And how did he learn that Kelso was his son? Doc would never have told him and it didn't seem likely that Emmaline would do so at this late date.

And speaking of Emmaline, how had she known that Kelso was her son? Now that Radine knew the truth she could see a trace of the woman in Kelso's features, but the resemblance wasn't strong enough for Emmaline to have noticed. Or was it?

The thought that Emmaline killed her own son to avoid a scandal made Radine's blood run cold. She would much rather believe it had been Bingham. But a picture of Emmaline watching Cinda at the piano during church service sprang to Radine's mind. The mother's expression had been one of such fierce and protective love that Radine had had to avert her eyes to keep from feeling like a peeping Tom.

Emmaline could even have thought she was protecting both of her children from making a fatal error, committing the most terrible sin. Perhaps she feared the two might marry in spite of being closely related and thought that such a sin might send them each to hell. A woman would do almost anything to protect her children from such a fate.

Not to mention protecting herself. After years of seemingly pious behavior as the wife of a minister of God, to be exposed as an immoral woman who had borne a bastard child would seem unthinkable. The family would have to leave Guthrie and their thriving church—perhaps moving so far as California to escape the scandal.

It was also possible that the passion for the daughter she had nursed and tended and joyously raised might be enough to cause Emmaline to smother a son she didn't even know. When it came to human nature anything was possible, Radine had learned.

She must next talk with Emmaline and then with Mr. Bingham. A shiver of apprehension ran down her spine. One of these was a murderer. And any person who would murder his or her own child wouldn't hesitate to kill a nosy housekeeper.

Chapter Eleven
Trouble Finds Radine

Radine's dilemma of deciding which suspect she should speak to first was solved when Luther Bingham came looking for her. She was at the desk in her tiny sitting room when there was a loud knock on the door. Expecting to see Sammy or Charity or Cook, she called out for the person to enter.

The next thing she knew a furious Bingham towered over her shaking his finger as if she were a naughty student and he the schoolmaster.

"You can stop running all over town discussing my business with tradesmen. My affairs are none of your business!" he shouted.

What had Harriet told her to do when a gentleman lost his temper? Oh, yes. Take control of the situation, she had said. If you can't think of anything else, offer him tea.

"I can see that you're very upset, Mr. Bingham. Would you care for a cup of tea to settle your nerves?" She forced herself to smile up at him sweetly.

Bingham's mouth snapped shut and he stared down at her, totally nonplussed. It suddenly seemed to dawn on him that he was behaving like a bully and raging at a petite and very pretty young woman. He stood speechless for a minute, as if disarmed and defused by her superior manners.

Radine watched as he pulled himself together. He straightened and moved his left arm to behind his back as she had often seen other gentlemen do when striving to be on their best behavior. Finally he cleared his throat.

"Forgive me for losing my temper, Miss Radine," he said. "But you have no business tricking the undertaker into telling you that I paid for young Kelso's funeral. If I chose to do a good deed then it's no one else's business."

His apology almost made her like him, and then she remembered that he might have killed Kelso. Radine's heart hardened toward him again. Harriet's lady-smithing lessons blew out of her mind, and she turned into a hard-scrapple prairie orphan once again.

"I've done nothing that I'm ashamed of, which is more than you can say for yourself."

The words sprang out of her mouth and echoed in the room. She stood, then glanced at the door knowing she may have put herself in danger. For sure she'd made a treacherous enemy. But she stubbornly refused to back down and stood toe to toe with the tall, imposing railroad executive. Her glare matched his. He might kill her, but he'd never bow her back.

Bingham's mouth gaped open. His anger disappeared and he looked both shocked and stricken. "I've done nothing to be ashamed of," he said.

Radine cocked her head to one side and raised an eyebrow.

He seemed to rethink his sentence. "No more than any other man who's made his own fortune, anyway," he said.

His words, meant to justify his behavior, fired anger through Radine. She thought of Kelso growing up alone and abandoned in an orphanage, and her mouth again flew open of its own accord.

"Are you telling me that any man would seduce an innocent young woman and then abandon her? Leave her to face the shame and the anger of her self-righteous father all by herself? I don't believe you."

Bingham blanched. "How did you...?" His mouth worked a few times, and then, to Radine's great surprise, tears formed in his eyes. He sank onto a straight-backed chair across from her. "I didn't know...." His voice broke and he dropped his head into his hands. He raised it a minute later to glare at Radine, his anger was back.

"If you say one word to hurt Emmaline, I swear, I'll..." He closed his eyes and seemed to struggle to get his emotions under control.

"Are you telling me you didn't know that you had a son?"

"Not until I spotted my grandfather's ring on his finger, then I knew what must have happened. That gold and ruby ring was the most precious thing I owned as a young man, and I gave it to Emmaline as my pledge of love. No matter how poor we were, my family held on to that symbol of better times. When I saw that ring on Nick's finger I *knew* he was my son."

The man was lost in the past. The small sitting room seemed charged with his emotion and Radine was almost afraid to breathe. Still as a mouse, she waited for him to continue.

"I never heard from Emmaline again. I learned she had married soon after I left, and I knew my dream of a life with her was over. So I threw myself into the railroad business and turned my energy to making money. When Emmaline and her family suddenly appeared in Guthrie I thought it would be best for her if I pretended that we had never met."

Unexpected pity touched Radine's heart. She bit her lip and listened as Bingham spoke again.

"Reverend Smith didn't meet me in Missouri. One morning in Guthrie he introduced himself to me. Emmaline was with him and we both pretended it was our first meeting. It was almost more than I could bear."

"And then Nick Kelso drifted into town."

"He did. I hardly noticed him at first, then one day he waited on me at the Emporium and I spotted Grandfather's ring."

"So you killed him to shut his mouth shut and keep him from ruining your reputation as well as Emmaline's?"

"No! I would never have hurt him—not ever. I have no other child. I wanted to give him a job but Hightower made him an offer he liked better."

The man almost convinced Radine, and then she remembered the chambermaid's tale of the quarter tip.

"Charity said you came down to the kitchen area at the same time as Kelso was murdered. She said it was to give her a special tip, but that didn't make sense. It puts you close by about the time Kelso was killed."

Sweat beaded Bingham's forehead, and his eyes pleaded in desperation.

"It's true. I came down to your room, but not to hurt the boy, only to talk to him and make sure he was healing properly. When I saw Charity I knew my presence would be hard to explain, so I gave her a quarter. But I left without going into your room. I swear it."

Chapter Twelve
Won't You Step into My Parlor? Said the Spider to the Fly.

Radine used some of her own hard earned cash to buy an apple pie to take to the parsonage. Cook didn't want her money, insisting that Madam Garrett would want her friend to be given the pie. But Radine stood firm. Right was right. She paid her quarter, put the pie in a basket, and walked to Emmaline Smith's house. She paused a minute before she knocked on the door. Nothing could have prepared her for her hostess' ravaged face.

Emmaline looked years older than she had just a few days ago. Her face was pale and pinched. She looked tired and there were dark circles under her eyes, as if she might have contracted a fatal illness.

"Hello Radine," she said, "If you wish to speak to my husband you'll find him at the church working on Sunday's sermon." Emmaline's smile didn't reach her eyes.

The woman's pain and her faded beauty were like an accusation to Radine. Why on earth had she ever promised to solve this murder? It was shameful for her to poke her nose into other people's business and reopen old wounds. Her usual quick tongue was struck dumb. Emmaline's eyes softened, as if she recognized Radine's embarrassment.

"Are you having more problems with your young man? Would you like to step inside and tell me what has happened?"

Radine wanted to shove the pie into Emmaline's hands and run like a jackrabbit back to the hotel.

Please don't leave. You got to ask her questions! I need your help.

Kelso's plea echoed inside her head. What on earth was she going to do?

"Please my dear, come in for a minute." Emmaline held the door open and gestured for her to step inside.

"I brought you one of Cook's fresh apple pies. I wanted to thank you for being so kind to me in the alley." Which was partly true. She stepped inside a darkened parlor. The formal and somber setting caused her to shiver.

"Come into the kitchen," Emmaline said. "That's my favorite room and I'll make us a pot of tea."

"Well, that's mighty kind of you. There's nothing homier than a cup of tea at the kitchen table." She followed her hostess back to a sunshine filled kitchen hoping to goodness that Luther Bingham was the murderer and not this woman.

"Sit down, my dear. While I make the tea you can tell me how things are between you and Micah. When I was a young woman I longed to have an older woman who could advise me. Like you, my own mother passed away when I was still a child but of course you have Harriet Garrett."

Radine sat on a straight-backed kitchen chair while Emmaline measured tea into a crockery teapot. Her hostess poured water from a steaming kettle already boiling on the back of the stove. *How on earth did I get myself into such a mess?* Radine wondered.

Unshed tears glittered in Emmaline's eyes and Radine opened her mouth to make an excuse and leave. Kelso stopped her. His voice spoke clearly inside her head.

I'm sorry to have put you in such a pickle, Miss Radine. This is a real nice lady and I don't blame you for running away. But Cinda is upstairs crying her eyes out, and I need you to give her my ring. And tell her that our love was the only good and pure thing that ever happened to me.

Radine blinked hard and just as suddenly as he had appeared, Kelso was gone.

"Do you care for sugar?" Emmaline asked.

"Sugar?" It took a minute for Radine to focus on anything as ordinary as sweetening her tea. "No ma'am, and I think I've stayed too long as it is. But if you don't mind, I'd sure like to speak to Miss Cinda before I leave." She saw Emmaline's spine straighten involuntarily.

"My daughter isn't up to having company today," Emmaline said. "She's suffering from a headache."

"Please let me run up upstairs for just a minute. I have a gift for her and I've got something important to tell her. It'll only take a minute and then I'll leave the both of you in peace. I promise."

Emmaline drilled Radine with a look that reminded her of her own mama, all those years ago. It seemed a long time before the woman answered.

"Very well, I'll take you to her."

Radine followed Emmaline up a narrow flight of stairs and then into a south bedroom. She knocked gently on the door then opened it.

"I'm sorry to bother you dear, but Radine Morgan is here and she insists on seeing you."

Cinda's pretty eyes were swollen by crying and her nose was red from being wiped with a lawn handkerchief, wet and crumpled in her hand.

Emmaline hovered over her daughter for a minute, looked hard at Radine, and then seemed to make up her mind. Without a word she walked out and closed the door behind her. This was a woman who understands about love, Radine thought.

Radine turned to Cinda, who had just sat up in bed.

"Nick died in your room." Cinda spoke softly, her eyes as large and as full of anguish as those of a wounded doe. "Do you think he suffered much?"

"No, there wasn't any pain." Radine didn't know if this were true or not, but it was the only answer she could give to Cinda. "And he talked about you much of the time."

"I can't believe he's gone." Tears ran down the girl's cheeks.

"He asked me to give you a message and a gift, if for some reason he didn't make it."

"He wrote me a note?" A glimmer of hope lighted Cinda's eyes.

"No, I'm sorry. It was a verbal message." Radine paused to clear her throat. "He said to tell you that your love was the only good and pure thing that ever happened to him."

Cinda smiled through her tears. "He was the most wonderful person I ever met. He asked me to marry him, and I intended to, no matter what Papa said. We were such good friends. I could talk to him about anything."

"Mr. Kelso also wanted you to have his ring." Radine pulled the beautiful gold and ruby ring from her pocket. She handed it to Cinda with the loop of ribbon she'd tied to it.

"This had belonged to his family. He said the women at the orphanage told him that. It was his treasure." She took the ring and pressed it against her cheek.

"I'm going to leave you now. Is there anything I can get you before I go? Would you like your mother to bring you a cup of tea?"

"No, I think I'd like to be alone for awhile. Thank you for coming. The ring and Nick's message mean everything to me." Cinda smiled through her tears. "First we heard that Nick was going to be all right and then suddenly he died. It's so odd that he left a message for me and instructions about his ring."

Radine stood speechless. She heard thunder and the sound surprised her. The sun had been shining when she left the hotel, now a storm seemed to be approaching. It seemed a bad omen. She shivered, trying to think of an answer for Cinda but for once she was speechless.

"Yes," she said. "It was odd."

"He must have had a premonition," Cinda said.

Chapter Thirteen
Dust and Other Devils

When Radine left Cinda and Emmaline, clouds covered the sun and the day seemed dark. Less than an hour before the sun had been shining. She frowned at the sight of a wall cloud just west of town. A storm would soon be overhead. The tail of a tornado could snake out of such a formation and rain seemed eminent. The weather had been dry lately and the farmers needed moisture desperately. What they didn't need was hail.

A wind gust billowed her skirts and she struggled to control them. About a mile away top soil whirled frantically in the center of a dust devil. She quickened her step and glanced toward the church. Should she shelter there until the storm passed? Just then Preacher Smith opened the door. He raised the kerosene lamp that he held in salutation and called out.

"Miss Morgan, there's a storm headed this way. Come inside until the worst blows over. You don't want to be caught outside if it hails."

That was true, but she was emotionally spent and couldn't bear anymore conversation just then.

The Bad Feeling swept through her but she wasn't sure how to interpret the warning. Should she go inside the church and escape the storm, or should she stay outside and brave the weather? She longed to be alone and wanted to head home, but should she?

"I'm sorry but I won't have time to chat with you," Pastor said. "I'm at a crucial point in my sermon and must keep working but perhaps you won't mind just resting for awhile?"

Thunder sounded and the rain started. Radine hated thunder storms. Both lightening and hail could be dangerous. Another bolt split the sky and thunder followed immediately.

That was too close! She made her decision and scurried into the church.

The glass kerosene lamp that Pastor Smith held flickered. He set it on a nearby table then closed the door, struggling against the wind. The smell of furniture polish and the fragrance of newly hammered pine lumber and the ink and pages of hymn books melded together for that familiar church smell that Radine loved. She paused, waiting for the usual feeling of peace to sweep through her. Instead, for no reason at all, she shivered.

Kelso's voice sounded in her head almost like a scream. *Get out of here! You're safer in the storm. Run away as fast as you can.*

Radine turned toward the door then stopped dead in her tracks. Preacher Smith's large frame blocked her path of escape. His face, always before genial, now seemed ominous, and his thin smile touched only his lips. He pulled a heavy-looking key from his pocket.

"I'll lock the door to make us secure against the storm."

What had she done? She'd forgotten this man was a husband and a father. Protecting his family might be more important to him than his love for God. Then she reasoned with herself. He couldn't be the killer because he hadn't been near her rooms at the time of the murder. Not one employee had mentioned his name when she had asked who was in the kitchen area on Saturday. Then her heart froze with remembrance.

Radine's talent for perfect recall flashed the exact conversation into her mind. She had asked if any unexpected visitors were around on the day of Kelso's murder. She had forgotten that Smith came to the kitchen almost every day in his effort to convert Cook. The preacher would have seemed invisible to the staff because he was always underfoot. *The preacher himself was a prime suspect.*

"You visited my home and disturbed my wife and daughter just now, asking questions about things that don't concern you, I presume."

His voice sounded so normal he might have been asking his congregation to turn to page 78 in the song book. Radine knew that her life depended on how she reacted. She flashed him what she hoped was a convincing smile.

"I took you and your family a freshly baked apple pie. I wanted you to have a special treat for supper." She kept her gaze steady, but she knew that she was a bad liar. "Now you just go on and write your sermon. I'm going to sit here in the back pew, quiet as a mouse, and pray until the storm passes." For the first time in her life, Radine decided to pray that a twister *would* hit.

"Don't bother to lie. I overheard your conversation with Doctor Johnson yesterday in his office."

"What?" Radine's heart turned to ice.

"I saw the two of you go inside and wondered if you might talk about young Kelso. I slipped quietly into the outer office and listened. Both of you have nice strong voices."

Radine's mind raced. She had to stall or divert him and somehow manage to escape.

"Aren't you worried that Mrs. Callahan will come by for prayer?" She named a church member known to frequent the Sanctuary. "If the door is locked she'll be worried. I suspect she'll go fetch the deputy."

Preacher's smile widened. Radine shivered against her will. The only thing she could think of was Micah. Why hadn't she accepted his proposal? Suddenly she knew that more than anything in the world she wanted to be his wife. The thought that they might never wed caused a grief so deep she touched her chest to quell the pain.

"I always pegged you for a sly one. No sensible woman would come out in this storm. Like all young women today, you don't know your place. You have brought destruction upon yourself."

He was going to murder her! Her mind raced to form a plan of escape. Then she heard someone try to open the door to the church. "Miss Radine?" a high boyish voice called. "I know you're in there, Miss Radine. Please let me in."

"Run Sammy!" she yelled. "Run away as fast as you can!"

Smith quickly unlocked the heavy door and then grabbed Sammy by the scruff of his neck and dragged him inside. The wind blew rain into the sanctuary.

"Hey! Let me go. I ain't done nothin'…"

Radine edged toward the table holding the oil lamp. She had to save Sammy, no matter what the price.

"Settle down you worthless scamp," Smith said, shaking the boy.

"You better not have hurt Miss Radine," Sammy yelled back and kicked Smith on his left shin. The preacher yelled and slapped Sammy hard.

Radine grabbed the oil lamp and threw it as far toward the pulpit as she could. At that moment she was grateful for a lifetime of hard labor, first in the fields as a child and later lifting and carrying heavy things at the hotel. Although small in stature, the muscles in her arms were well-formed and strong.

The lamp sailed about a third of the way into the church and crashed onto freshly varnished pews. Oil spilled and flames licked upward, red and furious.

"My church!" Smith screamed, releasing Sammy and stepping toward the blaze. "You've set my church on fire!"

Radine grabbed Sammy's hand and raced out the open door and into the driving rain. Instantly drenched and slipping in the wet mud, the two headed toward town. Suddenly Radine heard horse hoofs galloping toward them. She looked up to see Micah. He bent low in the saddle and encircled them both in his right arm, pulling the pair onto his saddle.

"Pastor Smith tried to murder us." Radine clutched Sammy to keep him from falling and pressed her cheek against Micah's chest. Never before had wet wool smelled so wonderful.

A shot sounded from the church and a bullet zinged past. She glanced back. Smith had a rifle aimed in their direction. Micah maneuvered his horse so Radine and Sammy were protected by his back, then raced away toward town.

Three hours later the church fire was extinguished and Pastor Smith was sharing Slick O'Reilly's jail cell. Radine sat beside Micah on Harriet's velvet settee with Sammy at her feet. Harriet rested on a sofa just across the way and Doc Johnson seemed satisfied that she was doing well. Zachariah handed around refreshments, homemade blackberry wine for the adults, for medicinal purposes he said. Sammy was delighted to be given cold ginger tea. Doc was the first to speak.

"I was wrong not to tell the deputy that Kelso didn't die from the stab wound. I see that now. At the time all I could think of was protecting poor Emmaline."

"So you did think she was the murderer?" Radine said.

"Yes, what with her terrible past and now facing the possibility that her two children might marry each other, I figured her mind became unhinged." He shook his head and sighed. "I figured the poor woman had already been punished enough, I wasn't about to send her to the gallows."

"How will Emmaline and Cinda be able to bear what's happened? Everything will be made public at the trial," Radine said.

"The trial will take place in Ft. Smith, which should help some." Micah patted her hand.

"I gave both of them sleeping powders to get them through tonight," Doc said. "And just as I was leaving I met Luther Bingham on his way in to check on Emmaline. They're still in love, you know."

"Will he have the courage to face such scandal? Will he treat Cinda Smith kindly do you think?" Harriet asked. Her past with the man hadn't led her to believe him to be of a generous nature.

"I think he'll surprise you," Doc said. "I'm used to sizing up men's intentions, and I saw pure steel in Bingham's eyes. His whole character seems to change when Emmaline is involved."

Radine smiled at the old man. She'd managed a few private moments with him earlier, and both had decided that it might be better if Cinda never learned the truth about who Kelso was. They agreed to hold their tongues forever and it seemed unlikely that either Emmaline or Bingham would mention the past. Some things were best never spoken of again.

There was a question Radine wanted to ask Sammy. She tousled his hair. "How did you happen to be at the church, young man? You were supposed to stay at the lumberyard."

Sammy ginned. "I was worried about you out in the storm so I went to see about you. You need a lot of looking after, Miss Radine. It's a good thing that Mr. Micah and I are both around."

"You're darned right, Sammy." Micah laughed. "When I saw that you were gone I started looking for you. Charity told me that Radine had visited the church so I knew that's where you'd be, too. The storm was about to hit so I followed you on my horse to bring you both home."

***

The next morning before Radine walked out to the pig pen to feed Esther, she donned her brand new hat. She could hardly wait to see Micah's face when she modeled it for him.

"Well, Esther, Micah and I have set a wedding date. It's to be on my next birthday, June 12, 1901. He said waiting a year would give me time to experience being a free woman and give him time to save money for a house." She lifted the stick and scratched the pig's head. "I told him that I was rock solid sure, but that waiting was fine. I want to have plenty of time to plan my wedding."

She thought back on the last few days and shook her head.

"I can't believe that it's been less than a week since this whole mess started. I sure hope that since I've solved his murder Nick Kelso will move on into the next realm."

Not without saying goodbye.

The hair stood up on the back of Radine's neck. Esther cocked her head and looked over Radine's left shoulder. You reckon that pig can see him? Radine wondered. But she was glad Kelso had stopped by one last time.

"Are you at peace now?" She asked.

Yes. And I'm real happy that Cinda and her mother will have someone to look after them. I'm ready to go.

Excitement sounded in Kelso's voice, as if he were now eager to be off on a new adventure.

"I'm going to miss you, Kelso," she said, almost regretting she would never hear from her invisible ghost again.

Lookie there down the alley.

Radine turned and saw Micah. "Hi there," she called out then waved. He grinned back and broke into a run to reach her more quickly.

But Kelso was already gone.

The Legend of Half Hollow Hill

Peggy Moss Fielding

For Susan Shay, who has joined my own private club (at least temporarily... it's called THE CANE CLUB.) My shirttail relative I appreciate and love

Peggy Moss Fielding

Chapter 1
April, 1920
Near Drumright, Oklahoma

"Is Oklahoma always hot in April?" Ellen held tightly to the side of the buckboard. Now I know why they're called buckboards, she thought, this feels as though it is lasting longer than the train ride from St. Louis.

Her driver turned his head toward her. She could see coal dust in each crease and ruffle of the silk of her white dress. Was that what he was staring at? She'd been stupid to wear her graduation dress on the train. She'd been trying to look all grown up.

"No ma'am. Sometimes it's hotter... and again it just might be snowing in April. This here is Oklahoma, ma'am."

"Can you tell me a little about the school or the community?" Ellen longed to ask the driver to slow down but she also longed to see the place that would now be home to her. She found herself shouting to be heard. "Why is the school called Half Hollow Hill School?"

Ellen watched tobacco juice fly over the side of the wagon then the man cleared his throat and looked at her again. He remained silent. Ellen tried once more.

"Mr. Linden, can you tell me why the place is called Half Hollow Hill?"

Again he cleared his throat. "Call me Jake, ma'am. Everyone around here does."

Ellen felt a prickle of irritation. Is he ignoring my question, she wondered, or is he just not hearing me? She tried again.

"Well Jake," she shouted the words, "Can you tell me anything about the school or about the house or the land? The lawyer in Drumright seemed to know very little about it."

"We'll be there in another hour." Jake spoke in a normal tone. "You can see everything for yourself then, I reckon."

Ellen realized she wasn't going to get any information about her new place. "I can't believe that I own a house and a school and *land*." She told herself for the hundredth time. "From Yahola Bigpond."

Ellen half shouted over the wagon noises, "I always believed that mother was making it up when she told me I had a cousin in Oklahoma, an Indian cousin."

Through the dust that swirled about the wagon Ellen could see pin oak trees, wild flowers and thick green grass. Not pretty and civilized looking like Missouri, she thought, but it had a kind of strange and primitive beauty.

An occasional rutted wagon road led off the dusty main trail. Ellen saw a rusty truck part way down one of the trails. Two men were putting pieces of wood under the back tires.

"Stuck," shouted Jake over the noise, "Horses is better back off in there. Them Tin Lizzies get into trouble way too easy."

"Where were they going in a truck?"

"Most likely drilling, somewheres up in there."

"Drilling? For oil?"

"Sure, for oil," again he grinned at his passenger. "I told you this here is Oklahoma. Onliest thing you gonna find around here is oil and Indians."

Ellen fell silent again. Everything seemed so strange. For a moment she felt a chill as if a cold wind had swept across her back. That's because I'm sweating," she assured herself.

The two rode in silence for the next half hour then Jake made an announcement.

"Me and Mary was talking about having you drink a cup of coffee or maybe some tea with us. How'd you like that?"

"Oh, Jake, right this minute I'd give five years of my life for something to drink." Ellen said and laughed.

Jake looked back over his shoulder.

"Ma'am, could I give you a little advice?"

"Of course, Jake. What is it?"

"Well, little lady, I wouldn't be so free with the words if I was you. Might be someone would be believing you."

Ellen puzzled over his words. "Did I say something wrong?"

"Reckon not. What I'm saying is don't be so free at giving up five years of your life."

Ellen laughed again. "All right Jake. I take back what I said but about that tea...?"

Jake grinned too. "See that little old shack over yonder to your left?"

Ellen nodded.

"Well that's me and Mary's place. I told her we'd likely stop and get us some refreshment before we went on to Half Hollow. How about it?"

"Wonderful. I'd love to meet your Mary and I'd especially like to try her tea, coffee or drinking water."

While Jake tended the horses, Ellen followed the tiny woman whom Jake simply introduced as, "This here's Mary."

"Ever been in a lease house before?" Mary pointed toward her front door.

"Is this a lease house?"

"Yes, or it was. Lease run out and the folks just moved on to the next field. Me and Jake is trying to do a little farming. We don't mind a lease house."

Ellen spoke carefully. "I am sorry, Mary, what exactly is a 'lease house' and why did the other people's lease run out?"

Mary laughed. "Your folks ain't oil people is they?"

"I guess I'd better try to become an oil person," Ellen said, "Jake tells me that there is nothing out here but oil... and Indians."

Mary became very serious. "And he is right, too. You'll see soon enough."

Ellen followed Mary into the unpainted one-room house. A corner of the room was curtained with sheeting cloth strung on wire. Their closet, Ellen realized.

"It ain't much but it's some better than living in a tent."

"Have you lived in a tent?"

"Oh, yeah. Me and Jake, we spent time in a tent over to Drumright when the boom first hit. I got used to it but I like living in a house better."

"This is what you call a lease house?" Ellen reminded the little woman of her question.

"Oh, yeah. When someone wants to drill on your land he gets a 'lease' from you. Give you some money to come onto your land and make a big hole in it. Iffen he finds oil you're both rich. Iffen he don't then you got the ruts he made and sometimes a little shack like this one here."

"You've made it very nice." Ellen hesitated a moment, "Have you seen my house? Is it a lease house?"

As Mary started to answer Jake stomped through the door. "Where's that there drink, woman? I'm parched right through."

Mary bustled about getting tea made. As she worked she talked to Ellen about her garden, their cow and about the pole barn that she and Jake were building. She explained that the pounding noise Ellen heard was the sound of the drill bit at the rig nearby. She said nothing at all about Half Hollow Hill.

"It must be a really dreadful place." Ellen murmured.

"What?" Mary stopped and stared at Ellen.

"Well, neither you nor Jake want to talk about my house. It must be really awful."

Mary looked at her husband. "Can't hurt to tell her about the house, Jake."

Jake nodded.

"Why, Miss Ellen, your house is just about the biggest, prettiest place around here," Mary spread her arms, "Almost bigger than the Fixico place on their ranch."

"Didn't you like Yahola? Is that it?"

"Oh, we liked Miss Bigpond, real good."

"Can you tell me what happened? All the lawyer in Drumright would tell me was that my cousin died in an accident."

Mary looked a question at Jake.

"Lawyer Grace Arnold," he murmured, "Miss Ellen visited the lady lawyer's office when she got off the train."

"Maybe you better find out from someone else," Mary said, "But you put your mind to ease about your house. All us in this neck of the woods is mighty grateful for the Half Hollow School. Miss Bigpond owned the land for the school, you know. She built the school house and then she taught in it."

"Do you have children in school?"

"We ain't got no kids," Jake put down his cup. "Just that we go to all the school doings. Box social planned for May...." His voice trailed off. "Before the... uh...accident."

"I don't see why we can't still have the social" Ellen leaned toward Mary, "That is, if you'll help me get everything ready. You have to remember that I just graduated from Normal School. This will be my first real teaching job."

"Why sure, I'd help. You *are* kinda young, ain't you?"

"I'm nearly eighteen."

Jake stood and urged Ellen to "Drink up." So they could get to Half Hollow before dark.

Outside, Ellen pulled herself up to the wagon seat and decided not to say one word to Jake unless he spoke to her, so the rest of the trip was made in silence. Ellen gripped the handhold more tightly as they neared her new home. "I'm afraid," she admitted to herself.

For a moment she thought wistfully of the pleasant house in St. Louis when her mother and father had been alive, then she remonstrated with herself. "You're lucky to have a place to go," she said half aloud.

"What's that?" Jake asked.

"Oh, nothing, Jake. I was just saying I'm ready to settle down after all this travel."

Silently Jake pointed to a large wooden structure about a hundred yards to the left of the road. She had seen a picture or two in the newspapers but this was the first time she had seen a real derrick, a drilling rig. Several men moved about the floor of the tall, almost lacey looking structure.

"Oh, Jake, could we go over and look at it?"

"Getting late," was all he said and he whipped up the horses.

Ellen stared at the strange edifice until the road curved, blotting the rig from her sight. At the last moment she saw a figure on the balcony-like construction at the top of the rig.

"A woman." She spoke aloud, "Jake, I think there was a woman up on that thing, I think she was calling out to us."

Jake didn't answer but he hit the horses again. "Git up there, you nags."

"That couldn't have been a woman," Ellen murmured to herself. "Not way up there." She shouted her question. "What do they call that little nest like structure at the top of the rig?"

"Monkey board," he said shortly then pointed through the trees, "That there's your place right up there ahead, little lady."

Excitement gripped Ellen. All thoughts of derricks, monkey boards and oil were driven from her mind by the wonder of at last seeing her own house and school.

"Are the children in school?" she strained for the first glimpse of the place.

"Not now," he answered, "Not since we ain't had a teacher."

Seconds later he pointed to a small log building, with a bell tower on top.

"Half Hollow School," he announced. He turned the wagon into a lane beside the school. "Your new house, ma'am," he gestured to the right with his whip, "Half Hollow Hill House."

The horses slowed and Ellen was staring at a large log building... what seemed to be two log buildings connected by an open porch like structure.

"Are those my houses?" Ellen rose to stand in the wagon as it moved sedately toward the small barn that was hidden in back of the house.

"All one house," Jake replied. "Pretty, ain't she? That dog trot do come in handy on these here hot days."

"Dog trot?" Ellen's voice quavered, "What's that?" She sank back onto the wagon seat.

"Don't worry, girlie," Jake spit over the side of the wagon. "You got a lot to learn but you got a lot of time to learn it in. Rest of your life, I reckon. A dog trot is a kind of a porch that connects the two parts of a house. Don't see too many of them up here in Oklahoma. Them as has 'em is old houses, probably Indian houses."

"Indian houses? I thought Indian houses were teepees."

Her thoughts were interrupted by the appearance of an old woman and an old man at the edge of the well swept yard.

"Who are they?"

"Them's your hired help. Uconthla Goat and her old man, Conzey Bucktrot. They come out to greet you."

The wagon rolled to a stop and Ellen stared down at the two brown faces that seemed to look not at her but above her. What am I supposed to do now? She nodded. "I'm Ellen Wiley," she said "Yahola Bigpond was my cousin. I'm going to live here."

Neither of the old people spoke.

"Jake?" Ellen turned toward the driver but he turned a closed face to her, also.

Her next words were almost a shout.

"I'm Ellen Wiley and I live here and I want to get out of this wagon and into a bath... right now!"

The old woman made a sign to the old man and he went to the back of the wagon to pull Ellen's trunk and suitcases out into the dust of the yard. Uconthla raised her hand toward the young woman still seated in the wagon and spoke at last. "You come."

"Yes, I have come and now I want to get down from here and get myself cleaned up," Ellen felt her temper rising. "Can you show me where I might get a bath?'

The old woman repeated, "You come."

Ellen turned to the back of the wagon. "Jake, do these people speak English?" she asked.

"Sure do," he replied, "She's trying to tell you to get on down from there and she'll take you on into the house and help you get settled."

Ellen directed a look of amazement at Jake but he grinned and spat tobacco on the ground. Ellen felt her good humor returning. "I come," she said... and stepped over the side of the wagon and jumped to stand in front of the woman.

"I Uconthla. He Conzey." The old woman then turned and started toward the log house. "Log cabin." She pointed toward the dog trot.

"This is no log cabin," Ellen answered, "It's way too big."

"Special house," said Uconthla, "Half Hollow Hill House."

Inside Ellen felt as overwhelmed as she had when she had first seen the place. The wide plank floors gleamed with wax and years of polishing. Heavy Turkish carpets were scattered about the floor of the room she had been led into. A high bed stood against one wall. Everything in the room was dark, heavy and expensive looking.

"This your room." Unconthla gestured. "Room of Yahola before."

"Thank you, Uconthla." Ellen's words were almost a whisper.

"Bring stuff now, then bath," the old woman gestured again. "You wait." She left the room.

Ellen stood rooted in the center of the room. Her gaze traveled to each piece of furniture... a wardrobe, a small desk, a well used rocking chair and the huge bed. A framed sampler hung on the wall at the head of the bed. Ellen stepped toward the sampler as the old woman reentered with Conzey and Jake and all her bags.

"Yahola do that," The Indian woman indicated the sampler, "She nine year old."

Ellen read aloud, "Home Sweet Home."

When Jake said, "Well, guess that's it. I'll be getting on back down the road." Ellen felt a pang of fear. She didn't want him to go and leave her here with these strange people in this strange house.

"Wait, Jake," she followed him out, "Do you... uh...that is, must you go... right now, I mean?'

He turned back. His smile was kind. "Don't worry little lady, you'll get used to everything. Me and Mary's right down the road, should you need us. This here is your place now."

"Thanks Jake, and thank Mary too."

She stood watching the wagon move completely out of sight before she turned and walked back to the dog trot and into the bedroom where the old woman stood waiting with a tin tub she had pulled into the room.

"Bath," the old woman said.

As Ellen bathed she could hear Uconthla and Conzey speaking words she could not understand. "I suppose I should try to learn their language," she said aloud but the warm water soothed her fears and she decided that perhaps things wouldn't be so bad after all.

The sun was setting before she was dressed and ready to start exploring her new home.

Uconthla came to show her to the dining room across from her bedroom. Again Ellen was surprised at the obvious luxury. The room was lighted by candles, rather than kerosene lamps.

"Old fashioned but very nice," she said to Uconthla.

"All nice here," Uconthla waved an insect away from the candle glow, "Everything better before but now, still nice."

"Can you tell me something about my cousin?"

"You not talk Yahola. Everything start new now. Roman Fixico say."

"But I'd like to know something about Yahola. How did she die? Where did she die?"

"You not talk Yahola."

Ellen fell silent. She ate the cold meat and salad but she felt the rising of the same discomfort she'd felt earlier. What had she walked into?

"I think I'll go to bed early," she told Uconthla, "Tomorrow I will see everything."

"Better not see everything."

"Uconthla, you might as well get used to it. I am now the mistress of this house and I plan to see everything tomorrow. Do you understand?"

"Understand."

During the night Ellen awakened. She saw bright moonlight from the high windows making silver rectangles on the floor of the room. I feel really rested, she thought, I think I'll walk out onto the porch... dog trot...for awhile. It's a beautiful night.

She pulled the heavy wooden door open and stopped cold. On the plank floor just in front of her door was the body of the old man, Conzey Bucktrot.

Ellen heard herself screaming. The sound lasted a long time and felt as if it came from a far distance.

Chapter 2

In the April sunshine Ellen couldn't understand the fright that had filled her at the sight of the man stretched in front of her door. "I thought he was dead," she whispered to Uconthla, "He was so still."

"Indian quiet." Uconthla whispered in return. "You noisey."

Ellen couldn't help asking why the old man had been set to guard her in the first place. Was it to keep her in or to keep others out? Uconthla wouldn't discuss the matter. She simply turned away. "Roman say," was her only comment.

Ellen put aside questions about why "Roman say" and who Roman was and what was going on. "I'm going to enjoy today," she told Uconthla, "I'm going to see my house, my school and my land."

Uconthla didn't try to dissuade her but through the exploration the old woman appeared in every room as Ellen made her rounds of discovery. The house was divided into sleeping rooms on one side of the dog trot and kitchen, dining room, parlor and library on the other.

The kitchen was huge, as were all the rooms. Ellen could hardly grasp the idea that the house and all the furniture were hers. The kitchen held a wood burning range as well as a fireplace built for cookery. In the corner of the room a small stove seemed out of place.

"Kerosene," murmured Ellen as she examined it. "Wouldn't this be cooler to cook on?"

Distaste thickened Uconthla's words. "No good. Cook on oil make food smell, taste bad. Oil bad for everything. I not use."

True, Ellen agreed inwardly, I've never liked food cooked over coal oil. It does have a taste. She nodded understanding.

"I'm going to the school, Uconthla. Have you a key?"

"No key."
"No key? No key for the house either?"
"No key."
In Ellen's room the old woman looked at the dresses hanging in the wardrobe. "All dresses too short."
"Oh, Uconthla, you're sounding like my mother. This is 1920. I know you like that long thing you're wearing but everyone in St. Louis and the rest of the country is wearing knee length dresses. I noticed Mary's dress was still long, also." Ellen felt a pinch of guilt. Women around here probably had to wear what they owned until they could get money for new things. She pulled on a yellow cotton dress she'd chosen for comfort. I guess I was lucky my parents wanted me to have stylish clothes. She felt the tug of loss at the thought of her parents.
"No corset?"
"No. No corset." Ellen laughed. "And you shouldn't wear one either. They say women are healthier if they can breathe freely."
"You be careful. Trouble."
"Uconthla, why are you constantly warning me?"
Without a word the old woman left the room. Ellen shrugged and finished readying herself for further exploration.
The walk through the side yard and across the lane was so normal, the sun so bright, the birds so cheerful, Ellen couldn't allow herself to dwell on Uconthla's behavior. I'll talk to her later. Maybe I need to apologize... later. Right now I want a clear picture of Half Hollow Hill. For a second she looked up at the hill that rose just back of the house.
"Of course," she murmured, "Caves."
The openings in the rocks were clearly defined in the bright light of the sun. I'll try to get up there today, too, she promised herself, but first, school. My school!
The school was smaller than the house but it was much larger than many country schools she'd seen in Missouri. The furniture seemed to have been made locally, but the desks and benches were nicely finished. The teacher's desk sat upon a low platform. Shelves on each wall to the side of the platform were filled with books. All the shelves were fronted with glass and each shelf had an individual lock.

Ellen ran her gaze over the books. She couldn't believe it. This rural school had more books and reference volumes than her classrooms in the big grade school in St. Louis had offered.

"The Book of Knowledge," she read aloud. The Encyclopedias from A to XYZ thrilled her, their dark green covers with gold embossed titles lent a scholarly look to the room.

She spread her arms and whirled in place. "If I can't teach here, I can't teach anywhere," she sang. I wonder how the books came here? Then wryly, I suppose the same way those Turkish carpets came to the house in the middle of a blackjack forest in Oklahoma. Magic, maybe? Uh huh. Money magic, for sure.

Drawers in the teacher's desk were clear of personal objects. In the center drawer she found the grade book. She turned quickly to the list of pupil's names. One Smith, five Fixicos, two Goats, one Bucktrot.

Jake was right, she mused, plenty of oil and Indians in our neck of the woods. A lump in the cover made her flip to the front. The bulge had been made by a needle which pierced the leather. The needle held an envelope addressed to her. Ellen Wiley was written in a fine Spencerian script.

For a moment Ellen sat unmoving. She recognized the writing. It was as if her dead cousin had reached out to touch her. Ellen's hands shook when she withdrew the letter.

To Ellen,
I know it is too late for me. He is coming for me in just a while. Everything I have done has been a mistake but there is nothing I can do about it. Maybe you, Ellen, my white cousin whom I have not seen, can save what is left. Use the Book of Knowledge. It will help in your work. It is new to our school this year.
Yahola

As Ellen began to reread the message she heard a footstep. She folded the paper to its smallest size. Using the desk as cover she unrolled the top of her silk stocking, wrapped the small packet into the silk and rerolled it into the above-the-knee position that had so shocked her mother. She smiled inwardly as she remembered her mother's horror at seeing her daughter wearing stockings rolled to the knee. She looked up. A man stepped into the classroom.

"I'm Merle Caudill, ma'am," he said, "I'm drilling just down the road. Maybe you seen our rig?"

"Mr. Caudill," Ellen rose to shake hands. His boots were heavy with oil and dust, but his trousers and shirt were clean, as were his hands. His dark blonde hair was combed straight back from his forehead. A thin red line etched across his forehead where his felt hat had rested. He held the hat in his left hand and reached for Ellen's extended hand.

"Pleased to meet you, ma'am."

"And I you, Mr. Caudill. I'm very interested in the drilling. My cousin never told me about an oil well being so close."

"Your cousin?"

"Miss Bigpond."

"Oh, yeah. She was your cousin?"

"Yes. I'm going to take her place here at the school."

The man stepped back and studied Ellen. "Yahola was mighty pretty but I think you got her beat, Miss... uh...?"

Ellen felt a ripple of flattery at the open approval.

"Wiley. Ellen Wiley. But please, we're neighbors. Call me Ellen."

"You bet. And you can call me Merle. I don't let nobody but pretty ladies call me by that name, neither."

"Oh? What do you let others call you?"

Ellen realized she was flirting with a stranger but she felt pleased with herself. She might really learn to like it here at Half Hollow Hill.

"They call me Dill."

Ellen smiled again. Nice to talk to someone who understood everything she said, someone who seemed to appreciate her. "In her letters Yahola never mentioned you. I wonder why?"

"Yahola wrote to you?"

"Oh, yes. We corresponded for some time before her accident." Ellen was silent for a moment. Maybe this man could give her answers to some of her questions. "Mr. Caudill... Merle... you were Yahola's friend. Can you tell me exactly how she died?"

"Well, I'm right sorry to have to tell you this, Ellen. Hope it won't influence your feeling about oil men." Merle frowned slightly. "She died over to my rig."

Ellen felt suddenly that she must sit down again. She moved blindly to the teacher's chair. "Exactly how did she die?"

"I can't tell you exactly, Miss Ellen. Some say she fell and some say she jumped."

Ellen closed her eyes. "You mean she committed suicide?" she whispered.

"Well, it might have been a real accident. Don't nobody know why she climbed way up into the rig. Most folks hereabouts think she jumped. Lawyer Grace Arnold said she thought Yahola did that, but for the sake of the community she and them other folks in Drumright called it an accident."

"No one knows why?"

"Nope. Them Fixicos is her cousins too, see. They all go through that mumbo jumbo about some kind of Indian curse or something. Listen. I think maybe that old squaw, Uconthla Goat is crazy, Ellen. Don't know as I'd want her doing for any of my sisters."

"What about Conzey Bucktrot? Is something wrong with him as well?" Ellen felt a slight wave of protectiveness toward the old couple but maybe this man knew them better than she did.

"Probably just a harmless old coot but you know them Indians is all related. They do whatever that Roman tells them to do. All the same clan."

"Who is this Roman everyone talks about?"

Merle walked toward the bookshelves and gestured toward the encyclopedias before he looked back at Ellen. "You looked at these books, yet?"

Ellen shook her head.

"Old Roman give all these books to the school. Last thing he give was them encyclopedias. Big man in this part of the state."

"Is Roman a chief?"

"Something like that."

Merle moved back to the desk to stand in front of Ellen. "You'll be meeting him soon enough. Just remember, them Indians ain't like us."

Ellen changed the subject. "Have you been up into the hills behind the house? I can see caves up there."

The oil man's teeth shone white in his sunburned face. "Like to explore your hills? I go up into the caves every once in awhile." He whirled his hat on his extended finger. "Fact is, I really come in here to talk some business with you. About that hill. Oil business."

"Could we do that some other time?" Ellen felt apologetic but she really wanted him to go. "Right now, everything is so new to me..."

"Oh, sure, hon." The driller answered. "I'd like to have a reason to come back." He leaned to put his face close to Ellen's. "Want you to think now about letting us have a lease on your hill area. We think Half Hollow Hill may be sitting on top of the richest pool yet."

Ellen felt a twinge of warning. What would Uconthla say about this offer?

Merle waved goodbye to her from the door. "Yeah, they tell me that there may be petroleum rock back up there all around them caves."

Ellen waved and smiled but her head felt full of the talk about oil. On her property. Did she want to be rich?

Ellen closed her eyes and put her hand to her forehead. Too much was happening. Seconds later when she opened her eyes she almost screamed. A different man stood in front of her. This was a tall, dark skinned man, broad shouldered, strong looking. His black hair was bound in two braids. He wore a cream colored silk shirt and a wide brimmed Stetson. His dark gaze seemed to impale Ellen.

Ellen's voice came out a squeak. "Who are you?"

"Roman Fixico."

Ellen stared. Surely the leader of the Indians was not this young? His unlined skin, and his lithe looking body seemed to be those of a man in his twenties.

"Are you the man who gave the books to the school?"

The man nodded but said nothing.

Why is he staring at me? Ellen asked herself. And why am I staring at him? Angrily she waved a hand at the benches before her.

"Won't you sit down, Mr. Fixico? It is bad of me to keep such an important man standing."

"You are angry."

"Not at all. I am perfectly used to having people stand and stare at me without uttering a single word."

"Pardon me for my rudeness, Ma'am." For the first time the young man smiled.

Be careful, she reminded herself. Remember what Jake and Merle said. Indians are different. But she felt herself returning the smile and staring at Roman Fixico.

"How did you get that unusual name? Roman, I mean." She watched the man slide into the small desk on the first row. She smiled inwardly to see him work to find a comfortable place for the long legs. His boots were well worn but they glistened with polish. Finally he settled for the aisle.

He took off the hat, then looked at her and grinned. "The teachers at the Indian School used to crack me across the knees for this."

Ellen laughed with him. "It is you who must excuse me, Mr. Fixico. I have been rude to you. I've heard your name from every person I've met since I arrived, but I didn't expect anyone like you. My name is..."

"Ellen Wiley."

"Oh, have you heard about me, as well?"

"Yes, and I have written to you, also."

"Of course. The letter that told me I was needed at Half Hollow Hill. I thought it was from the lawyer. She had written earlier but she didn't ask me to come. Then I got your letter... with no name on it."

Roman Fixico's smile disappeared. Again the look of intense study swept across his face. "You are Yahola's cousin."

"I think you know that, Mr. Fixico. Her father was my grandfather's brother. Her father came to the territory and married Yahola's mother. We never met, Yahola and I, but we knew about each other. We wrote."

"She was my cousin, also." Roman spoke in a voice so low that Ellen had to lean forward to hear. "She had something of me in her and something of you as well. You would have liked her."

"Is it true she killed herself?'

As if a mask descended upon his face, Roman Fixico was once again the frightening stranger she'd first seen.

"The man, Merle Caudill was here."

It was a statement, not a question.

"Yes. Did you see him?"

"I do not need to see him. He leaves his scent."

Ellen felt her face reddening. What a maddening, hateful man this was. He seemed to think he was some sort of Lord of the region. Well, not at Half Hollow Hill, he wasn't. She could be as stubborn as he was!

Both sat in silence for what seemed like hours to Ellen.

Finally he smiled again. "You will do well."

But Ellen was not to be appeased. "Thank you so very much, Mr. Fixico. I was waiting to hear whether I passed your royal examination or not. Now I can sleep tonight!"

The man laughed again and left the school room without another word, laughing as he went. On the porch he replaced his dove colored hat. Still laughing, he strode toward his horse.

Ellen tossed her head and went on with the inventory of the supplies in the building. Everything seemed in good order. Only one thing was missing, one volume of the Book of Knowledge, the volume labeled "R."

Chapter 3

At the midday meal Ellen toyed with her food. She already felt full of sights and sounds and experiences.

"You not eat."

"Sorry, Uconthla. Maybe I'm still too excited."

"You make trouble."

Ellen stared at the Indian woman, her eyes widened with anger. "Why is it that everything you say sounds like you're giving me orders? Don't you work for me?"

"I take care you."

"Whoa. You are hired to work here... aren't you?"

The woman's face seemed made of stone. "You make trouble. You talk with man. You stick your face in everything. You not listen."

Ellen sighed.

The woman stared impassively, as though waiting for Ellen's words.

Ellen sighed again. "Uconthla, I'm sorry. We just aren't talking about the same things. Tell me... did Yahola hire you to work in the house? If she did I'm willing to make the same arrangement. That does not include consulting you about my private life."

A strange gleam appeared deep in the eyes of the old woman. "I stay. I take care you."

Ellen screamed. "I don't want to be taken care of!"

"I care for Half Hollow Hill also. This special place. Conzey and me, we stay here. For all Creeks. Our tribe."

Ellen threw her napkin on the table. "There really is no use talking to you, is there? I think Merle was right. You are crazy."

Uconthla's dark eyes burned now. "Merle!" she spit out the word. "This Merle crazy. You no talk Merle."

Ellen shrank back from the next venomous whisper. "You no talk Merle."

Ellen stood without speaking and walked through the living room, and out the door opening onto the dog trot. She met Conzey as she strode across the wide porch to the path that led across the meadow. "Schoolhouse," she said shortly and walked on before the old man could say anything. In the schoolroom she loosened the tightly rolled top of her silk stocking and removed the folded envelope. She reread the message from Yahola.

She worried over the sentence saying it was too late, before refolding the note. She looked up in astonishment. "Of course," she whispered.

She yanked open the desk drawer and scrambled about inside. Where were those keys?

In seconds she had the heavy ring in hand and was balanced on a student bench trying each key in turn. The third key opened the shelf where the encyclopedias rested. She loaded all the green backed books onto the teacher's desk. She stepped up on the bench again and stared at the blank wooden top, sides and back of the bookshelf. Nothing.

"But there has to be something," she breathed, 'That's what she meant in the note. That she left something else for me." She swept her hands over every inch of the shelf. Still nothing. Solid wood.

She stepped down and began replacing the tall books. When she'd replaced more than half the volumes she stopped.

"In the books themselves," she said and began riffling the pages of the book she was holding. No note, no paper, nothing fell out. She sighed. She'd been so sure Yahola had left her a message in the encyclopedias. When all were back in place she stared at them as if trying to force them to give up the secret she was still sure they contained.

"Read," Ellen repeated, as if she'd just heard the word. She pulled the first volume from the shelf and began to read. She read for several minutes then smiled and looked up to the place where she had seen...or heard the word, "Read."

"I've got it, Yahola," she said, "It will take a little time but I know how to do it now."

A flash of white at the window caught her eye. A young woman's face appeared. Waist length black hair moved softly in the spring breeze. The woman's white shirtwaist was pinned high at the neck with a peach colored cameo. She smiled and spoke but Ellen missed the word.

"Come on in," Ellen called.

The woman didn't move from the window. She smiled and spoke again. Her speech was again inaudible.

Ellen ran to the door to call her visitor into the room but there was no one. She moved all the way around the building but still she saw no one.

"It's getting dark," Ellen spoke aloud. She looked once more at the window and shivered. She scooped up the "A" volume and literally ran for the house. The idea of being alone in her bedroom made her shiver again so she headed for the warm kitchen where at least there was another human being.

Uconthla stood at the great black range stirring something. As she stirred she made sounds. Soft guttural sounds. She did not turn when Ellen entered the room.

The old man sat on the floor, in the corner of the kitchen. His eyes were closed. He did not look up.

"What are you cooking, Uconthla?" Ellen asked brightly.

The old woman did not stop stirring nor did she stop the wordless chanting.

"I've been working at the school. I saw a young woman...." Both old faces turned toward Ellen, "She was really pretty. Her hair was down and blowing in the wind."

"What she look like?"

"Oh, well, Indian, I guess. Long black hair, high cheekbones. She was wearing a white shirtwaist and a pinkish cameo at the neckline."

Both old people spoke in unison, "You talk her?"

Ellen stammered, "Well, she talked, uh, no, I guess I didn't talk to her. Or she didn't really talk to me. She was talking then she was gone..." Ellen tried again, "Well, she was gone when I ran outside to speak to her."

"She come to you." Uconthla put down the spoon she was holding.

"What do you mean?"

Conzey spoke in a high singsong. "Yahola come back. Little Yahola come back. Help our people."

"Yahola!" Ellen's voice held shock even she could hear. "Yahola is dead. The person I saw was real."

The old people spoke to each other in Creek. Ellen heard Yahola's name mentioned several times.

"What's going on?" Ellen spoke more loudly than she had intended. "What are you two talking about?"

"You will help lead our people."

Ellen's breath huffed out with exasperation.

"Listen to me, Uconthla, and you too, Conzey. I don't want to hear anything about your superstitions. Please don't try to involve me in your rituals."

"Half Hollow Hill our ancestor home," Uconthla announced.

"Now you owner Half Hollow Hill," said Conzey.

"Yahola our 'special protector,'" Uconthla gestured in the air.

"She come to you after death," Conzey nodded at Ellen

Ellen used her best school teacher voice. "Now you two... Don't. Say. Another. Word. You are both acting very strangely indeed... and I am going to bed."

In moments Ellen lay wide eyed in the big soft bed, watching the silver rectangles grow larger on the floor of her room. She wondered if she were the one who was either sick or crazy.

"Oh, God, I *did* see her," Ellen spoke aloud. "I've seen her twice.

Chapter 4

Next morning, after toast and coffee, Ellen sat at the desk in her bedroom to find Yahola's message within the "A" volume. "I'm getting as dotty as everyone else around here." She threw the book to the floor. "What I need is a good dose of normality."

She hurried through dressing and combing her hair. "You look sane," she spoke to the image in the mirror, "How about a visit with the oil man? After all, you were invited." Her reflection dimpled and she answered herself, "Don't mind if I do!"

She dashed to the kitchen to tell Uconthla where she was going. "And I don't want Conzey following me. You tell him." She waited until she heard Uconthla speak to the old man in Creek, then she added, "I'm going to walk... by myself."

Uconthla stared at her for a long second, then said only, "You make trouble."

The trail was quiet except for the distant pound and lift of the cable tools. She watched brownish dust sift over the white kid leather of her slippers. She should probably get some hightop shoes to wear for hiking around here. Both Mary and Uconthla wore high topped shoes.

"These are my graduation shoes," she said aloud and giggled. She knew she'd wanted to impress the driller. Somehow the strange happenings of Half Hollow Hill didn't seem so important while she was walking in the sunlight on a dusty road to visit an oil-well-in-the-making.

A horse and rider emerged from the heavy brush beside the narrow road. Ellen gave a soft sound of fright then lifted her chin and walked faster when she saw the rider was Roman Fixico. His horse was huge. Yeah. A horse would need to be big to carry such a tall, muscular man

The black horse pranced in the dust beside her. The tall rider did not smile but he swept off his broad brimmed hat and bowed low over the saddle horn.

"Good morning, Miss School Teacher."

Ellen began to run.

"Are you trying to outrun my horse?" the young Indian leaned down and easily swept Ellen up to sit in the saddle in front of himself.

For a moment Ellen was silent with shock. The ground looked far away below her two white slippers. She exploded in a fury of words and fists.

"How dare you? You savage!"

Ellen pounded the large man's thigh but he held her closely enough that she could touch him nowhere else. With her right arm she pounded the neck of the black monster she sat upon.

"Sh, girl. Now don't hurt my horse. Hush. I just want to show you something."

"Let me down this instant!"

"If I let you down will you promise to let me show you something? Will you listen?" He made a slight movement and the horse stopped moving. He whispered into Ellen's left ear. "I'll go down first then I'll bring you down. Okay?"

"Oh, all right. Hurry! This horse is way too big."

Fixico stood down on the left side of his animal, while Ellen clutched the saddle as tightly as she could. "Let go," he spoke gently, "I can't bring you down unless you loosen your hold on the saddle." Ellen reluctantly held her hands out to the man. "See?" He held her about the waist as he let her slide down his body. For a second she couldn't say a word but could only stare up into his dark gaze.

"Come. We will walk together. Tiger will follow us..."

"Tiger?"

"My horse is Tiger. We Creeks like the name. Did you not walk up Tiger Hill when you were in Drumright to see the lawyer?"

"How did you know I saw a lawyer?"

They trailed through the narrow path through the trees and brush, Roman leading, the monster horse following Ellen, occasionally cropping grass as he walked.

"Perhaps you will learn that I know all that you do."

"Uconthla," she muttered under her breath.

"Uconthla...and others," he smiled back at her frown. "That is the way it is in a family."

"I'm not your family."

"True. Now let us be silent until we reach the stream."

Soon the man, the girl and the horse emerged at the edge of a small stream. Roman pointed upward toward the sound of the drilling.

"The greed for oil spoils our world," he said.

Ellen looked at him a moment before answering his comment. "And, I guess, Mr. Fixico, you have your share of that greed. I see you in a silk shirt each time we meet...shirts not made in Drumright, Oklahoma, maybe in London or New York or some such place. Very expensive."

She reached to touch his dove colored hat.

"Your hat cost more than I will make in one month as a teacher. Didn't the money you use for such items come from oil?"

"You are right, Miss Wiley. We are not totally without blame. We too, when we saw our lands and our animals taken from us, we wanted something...so we settled for what the white man finds important...oil money."

"See, teacher?" Roman stirred the water of the stream with a long stick. "See the rainbows in the water? Are they beautiful to you?"

"What is that?"

"Oil. Tiny drops of oil that coat the surface of the water and stain the rocks and that will eventually kill the fish and other water creatures."

He turned away from the stream. "We cannot drink this water anymore. Nor can Tiger. The taste is no longer sweet." His voice held sorrow.

He turned to face her and seemed to look into her mind.

"Half Hollow Hill is the heart of our special land, resting place of our ancestors. Who lives in that place becomes caretaker for our past."

"But I'm not Indian."

"You were chosen by an Indian." The words were cold.

Ellen shivered. Why did the place that had seemed so exciting, so wonderful, so promising an hour ago, now seem frightening? She stared upward again at the brown face that loomed above her.

"He is threatening me," she told herself. Aloud she said only, "Yes, Yahola did leave the place to me. Now, I think I'll just go back to it."

She turned and started back the way they had come. The man and the horse did not follow her. She forced herself to walk all the way even though she was desperate to run. When she arrived at the house she ran into the kitchen. When she spoke she could hear the quaver in her own voice.

"Uconthla, never do that again."

"What do?"

"I know you sent Conzey to get that Roman Fixico," she shouted. "For the last time what I do is no concern of yours." She turned to leave the kitchen. She heard the words the old woman whispered, the words followed her.

"You belong us."

I don't have to stay here, she told herself, I can walk to the school. I'll take the 'A' volume and really concentrate on what Yahola was trying to tell me.

Before beginning work Ellen pulled a large sheet of heavy paper from a shelf and crayoned a message on it. She tacked the paper to the school building wall that faced the road. The poster read, "Box Supper. Saturday Night. 7:00. Tell your friends. All are invited. Miss Wiley."

Ellen stepped back and admired the red lettering.

"They can see that from the road," she said aloud then turned to go back inside. She'd like to get to know all her neighbors, not just the crazy ones.

As she worked at the desk she could feel her excitement rising.

"I'm beginning to understand," she whispered, "Yahola was sending a message just to me." As Ellen worked she wrote down the letters and words. She then erased every trace of the very light lettering or underling from the books.

She meant me to do it this way. Even though she was desperate she was taking care of the new encyclopedias. She must have been very proud of her school.

The message told of meeting "him" secretly, of being under his spell, of the worry that she had because she had betrayed a trust, and last, of fear for her own life.

When it became too dark to work on the message, Ellen slipped across to the house. She glanced at the red streaked sky above the hillside. The caves weren't visible because of the setting sun behind them.

"Half Hollow Hill!" she said to herself. She had an impression of hills grasping for her. She ran into her own bedroom and stood trembling when she finally closed the door. She felt as if she could again hear Uconthla's whisper.

"You belong us."

Chapter 5

She worked late Thursday evening. The shadows on the walls of the school lengthened even further as she transcribed words and letters then erased the marks. She whispered each word with a kind of secret triumph. When the classroom finally grew too dark she looked about with puzzlement.

"What am I doing in a place called Half Hollow Hills?" She asked aloud. For a moment she thought she heard a sound in the darkened room. She bolted from the school to reach the safety of the lamp lit kitchen.

Ellen relaxed into her chair and laughed a bit at her own fears when she heard the old woman say, "You eat." Ellen felt as though Uconthla had handed her a small gift labeled "Security."

Later, in the bedroom Ellen felt shame. "I'm acting like a child," she told herself, "I'm beginning to see and hear something frightening everywhere. Tomorrow I really must get to work readying the schoolhouse for the party and for opening school." With that thought she snuggled into the feather mattress and slept.

Voices penetrated her sleep. She opened her eyes and watched the sunbeams curling through the air above her. Again she heard voices. "Mary and Jake." she decided, "Talking to Conzey." She pulled on her robe and moved to the doorway. For a second she watched the two white people talking and laughing with the old Indian man.

"I'm awake," she called. "I'll be dressed in two shakes. Conzey, please tell Uconthla that Mary and Jake will have breakfast with us." In moments Ellen was dressed and embracing Mary and shaking hands with Jake.

"I'm so glad to see you two."

"Saw your sign a day or so, back. Told Mary you was going on with plans for the box supper. Folks hereabouts is talking on it some."

"I come over to help you get ready," Mary said, "Soon as we get a cup of coffee with you, me and you can get right over to the school house and get that place cleaned and prettified for tomorrow night."

"Oh, Mary" Ellen lowered her voice to a murmur, "I'm so glad you came. I'm simply desperate to talk to another woman."

"Can't you talk to Uconthla?"

"Well, of course, there is Uconthla... but she's so strange... and anyway, I know you understand what I say and I understand everything you say."

"Don't you let them fool you, honey." Mary glanced about to see that the old couple were busy elsewhere. She laughed. It was an uncomfortable sound. "Them old Indians may not talk the way we do but they understand most everything we say... and do, for that matter."

Ellen was silent for a moment. Her voice when she spoke, was almost a whisper. "Oh, Mary, the other night Uconthla said to me, 'You belong us.' She kind of hissed it at me. What does she mean? Sometimes she scares me to death and sometimes she seems like a mother to me. What do you think?"

Her visitor looked over her shoulder and then back at Ellen. "I think you and me better get us some rags and soap and get on over to fall into that work."

Neither she nor Jake like to talk about anything that touches on the Indians. Why is that? Ellen shook the questions from her mind and followed Mary to the kitchen. Mary's banter and Uconthla's laughing replies sounded strange in Ellen's ears. This kitchen isn't used to laughter, she thought.

In the classroom the fun of working with Mary seemed to make the sun shine more brightly through the long windows. Flowers on every shelf scented the classroom. Ellen moved with the rhythm of the work and found herself talking and laughing and even singing.

By evening, when Jake and Mary waved goodbye from their wagon, Ellen hummed as she walked back to the house.

Uconthla had placed lighted lamps in nearly every room of the house and the log building seemed a joyous haven.

"When I get to teaching I won't have time for all this nervous brooding I've been doing," Ellen told herself, "Work is the answer."

Toward evening when Ellen saw people beginning to arrive she hurried to get ready.

"No short dress," Uconthla ordered.

Ellen smiled agreement and chose her newly clean graduation dress, her longest. It fell two inches below her knees as her St. Louis school had required.

When she was ready to go she picked up the box packed with Uconthla's chicken and fried apple pies. After she'd put the ribbons on the box she swung the box in one hand and hummed as she walked. Inside, for just a moment, she savored the clean, pleasantly scented room, then she carried her yellow box to the table at the front of the classroom. She fluffed the bow of pale green ribbon which sat atop the box and looked around the room once more before she moved to the front door toward the waiting crowd.

"I'm Ellen Wiley," she called, "Welcome to Half Hollow Hill School. Please come on in."

She watched the women put their decorated boxes on the table next to her own. Everyone talked and laughed. She could see her neighbors were having a good time with each other and she responded when they spoke to her, but she could hear little of what they were saying. She looked at the far window where the young woman from her dream had stood...and there she was...visible in the early evening twilight.

"Oh, there she is," Ellen spoke aloud. She walked to the wide front door of the school and looked outside to the place where she had seen the woman. "Where'd she go?" Ellen looked back at the crowd in the room. "That young woman was here the other day and when I went to invite her in she disappeared. Now, she's gone again."

Ellen turned to the woman nearest the door.

"Didn't you see her?"

When the woman didn't answer Ellen continued. "I think she lives down near the rig. That's where I first saw her."

The people in the room fell silent. No one moved.

They look like a photograph, thought Ellen. She took a step to the porch of the school. Mary followed and closed the door behind them. As the door closed Ellen could hear sounds break loose as if on signal.

"The new teacher saw her."

"We don't know who she saw." A man's voice.

"The teacher's really a stranger..."

"Yahola's cousin..."

Mary pulled at Ellen's arm to move Ellen down into the school yard. "Come on, honey, let's walk. Don't mind them."

Ellen followed like a dazed child. "What happened, Mary? What did I say that was wrong?"

Mary stopped and faced her. "You got to be careful, Ellen. You being the new teacher and all..."

"Careful? Careful of what? I don't understand."

Mary answered in a whisper. "Ain't no use stirring up the folks. Gossip'll get you into a lot of trouble."

"Gossip!" Ellen gasped.

"Well, talking about her coming to the school house."

"But that isn't gossip. There really has been a young woman here. I've seen her three... no, four times. All I wanted to know was who she is."

"Don't you know?"

"Of course not. I've never talked to the woman. Is everyone in Oklahoma, crazy?"

Mary looked out into the darkness of the school yard, then back at Ellen. She stepped closer to Ellen.

"The woman you've been seeing? That's Yahola."

Chapter 6

"Don't be silly." Ellen smiled to take the sting from her words. "Yahola's dead. Come on. Let's go back to the social."

The lamplit room seemed brighter and noisier when Ellen followed Mary into the classroom. Jake was holding up a red box trimmed in white.

"One dollar," came from the back of the crowd, and Jake handed over the box Ellen stood and watched then glanced at the table, then away. Her yellow box hadn't been sold.

At that moment Jake's left hand closed around the edge of the yellow box. His right hand flicked the green ribbon perched on top. "Looks like a educated hand decorated this here box. Pretty, ain't it? What am I bid?"

Several people laughed. One man shouted, "You can get some learning along with that there supper."

A gray haired Indian man called, "Fifty cents for that."

"Come on now, this here is prime good food. I can smell it." Jake lifted the box toward his face. "Worth more than four bits."

"Six bits."

"A dollar."

"Two dollars."

Ellen looked toward the last bidder. His dark face seemed carved of polished rock.

"Roman Fixico," she whispered.

Mary elbowed Ellen's arm. "They gonna have a bid war on your box."

"How do you know... how do they know it's mine?"

"Why hon, everybody recognizes their wife or girlfriend's box. You're the only newcomer here. Got to be yours."

"Ellen heard, "Five dollars," from the far side of the room.

"It's that driller, Caudill," Mary murmured.

"Six dollars," from Roman.

"Oh," Ellen whispered, "That's too much money."

"Worth it to them two, I guess," Mary answered, "School gets the money. Let 'em bid."

Ellen missed Merle's next bid but the whole room heard Roman Fixico's clear, cold, "Twenty dollars."

Jake gasped, then smiled and turned toward Merle. "Anyone else? Want to make it twenty-five?"

Merle smiled also, then waved his hand in a negative motion. "Too rich for me."

"Sold to Mr. Fixico. Reckon you'll be eating dinner with the schoolmarm, Roman." Jake handed the box to the young Indian man. "And I think you got yourself a bargain."

Mary put a hand on the small of Ellen's back and pushed Ellen forward. "Go on. You got to have supper with him since he bought your box."

Ellen moved one step toward the man, then stopped.

"Go on," Mary urged. She gave Ellen another push.

Ellen walked to face the man. She took the yellow box from his hand and moved toward the door. "Let's eat outside," she called over her shoulder. Roman Fixico followed silently.

Hand on the doorknob, Ellen turned and smiled. "Steps?" she asked. He nodded.

I won't be the one who speaks first, Ellen resolved inwardly. I'll die before I talk...unless he says something first. She watched the man's hawk-like profile from the corner of her eye as she took out napkins, then fried chicken, followed by fried pies, and still no words came. Finally she could stand it no longer.

"Pretty night," she spoke loudly into the silence.

"Um," came the answer from beside her, then silence again. Moments passed, both ate.

Ellen threw a half eaten chicken leg back into the box.

"I might as well be eating by myself," she said, "What's wrong with you?"

Roman turned to look at her. Surprise mixed with amusement sounded in his voice, "Wrong with me?"

"You've eaten almost your whole meal, two pieces of chicken and even a fried apple pie, without one word."

"I beg your pardon, Miss Wiley."

"Ellen."

"I beg your pardon, Ellen. I've forgotten my white manners. I've been too long with Indians. We eat in silence."

"Oh. I didn't know."

A brown hand gestured toward the hills behind the school. "I was thinking about the hills there. Half Hollow Hill is important to us." He reached for another pie.

"To 'us?' Who is 'us?'"

"Important to our tribe, I should say."

"Not *our* tribe. *Your* tribe, Mr. Fixico."

White teeth gleamed in the darkness. "Roman," he corrected softly.

"Why are my hills important to the Indians... uh... Roman?"

"This is sacred ground." The tanned face turned toward her again. "Our past lies buried here. Our ancestors live in Half Hollow Hill. Their spirits walk all about us. The caves above hold many secrets." His voice stopped for a moment then he added, "Now *you* are the one who keeps this sacred place."

"Me? I'm keeping the Indian's sacred place?"

"All of this." He moved his hand again. "All sacred. All given into your keeping. Yahola meant it that way, Ellen."

Ellen made a sound, her heart seemed to lurch toward the man who continued speaking.

He laughed softly at the sound. "All... all... given into the lovely hands of Miss Ellen Wiley."

They sat for a moment more in the silence of the warm Oklahoma evening, then Roman continued

"The 'old meeting place' is gone. Where the ugly derrick now sits was the place where our tribe met each year... now, no more. We have 'oil rights' instead." His voice held an edge, "The rig, the men, the noise... all intruders."

"Does everyone feel the way you do about drilling? You're getting lots of money." Ellen touched the shirt sleeve nearest her. His arm flexed under her fingers.

"'The rigs are an abomination...'"

As Roman spoke the door opened and light flooded the steps.

"Hey, little lady, you going to stay out here all night?"

"We were just chatting, Mr. Caudill. Come on out and join us."

"Us? I don't see no one here but you, little lady."

Ellen felt strangely saddened. The beautiful man with the compelling voice was indeed gone without a word, in the second she had turned to look at Merle.

"Well, I thought I was talking to Mr. Fixico. Come on and sit down. Maybe he'll be back in a minute."

"I been wanting to talk to you. We don't get many pretty ladies like you out here, Miss Ellen. I been wanting to talk to you about something else."

"What's that?"

"About your place here." The driller seated himself on the step. "I was wanting to talk about a lease on your place."

Ellen felt the closeness of the man. Heat radiated from his body and seemed to envelope her own. Almost involuntarily she moved to leave a space between them.

"Why do you want to lease my place?"

The oil man looked down at her. "Kinda skittish, aren't you? Let's not talk about them leases now. Let's talk about us, what say?"

Ellen felt blood rising in her face. She could almost hear what her mother or her friends back home would say about the two men who had shared the step with her tonight. They'd say "suitable" and "unsuitable" she thought, common sense would tell a girl which would be the better choice for a friend.

"Oh, Merle, I'd rather talk about leases," she said.

Chapter 7

Ellen called goodnight until all the wagons and horses were gone. She heard crickets singing in the darkness outside. "Good night everyone," she called once more toward the sound of hooves. There was no answer and silence engulfed the school. Ellen shivered.

"Cool tonight," she said aloud. She moved into the classroom and turned down all the lamps then blew them out. At the last lamp she paused for a moment. "Should I carry it to the house?" She asked aloud.

"Don't be silly," Her answer scoffed at her fears. "You know the way," she murmured, and she broke into a half run toward the log house. No lamps were lighted in the kitchen, nor in any other part of the house.

"Uconthla!" Ellen called. No answer.

"Strange," she said aloud, then she called again, "Uconthla, Conzey." Again, no answer. She stood in the open dog trot and looked up at the hills behind the house. The rounded mounds were a darker blackness against the dark sky. The stars seemed to glitter more brightly as she stared upward.

"That's not a star," she whispered. That's a light." For a moment she held her breath and peered at the light which was joined by another, then two more.

"Why are you up there?" She asked in her normal tone, then she shouted, "Uconthla, Conzey, are you up there?"

The lights disappeared.

Ellen watched and listened a moment longer, then she sighed and headed for her bedroom.

I'm stupid, she thought, I should have explored this whole place by now. I don't even know what's up there... except for those stories Roman Fixico told me.

Later, after sleep had claimed her, her legs twitched as in her dream she tried to move from the place where she had first seen her cousin. She saw a light. The light moved nearer and a woman's face came close to Ellen's. "You must go back now," the woman said.

"You're the one I've seen," Ellen said, "You're the woman with the long black hair."

"Yes," The woman smiled and pointed into the distance. "Go back to the school now."

Ellen turned in the bed and felt herself awakening in the dark room. The high windows in her bedroom wall glowed red. "What?" Ellen murmured in newly awakened confusion. "Is that a fire?"

She threw back her quilt and raced for the door. "It is a fire. The school," she shouted, "The school is on fire." She ran across the yard toward the other structure. "The school's on fire!" She screamed the words as she ran.

Chapter 8

Distance to the school seemed to grow rather than diminish and her cries mingled with the beat of horse's hooves and men's shouts. Ellen's words exploded from her lungs.

"Hurry. The school is on fire."

Figures of three men on horseback seemed to dance in and out of the light from the flames which caught now at the bottom of the front door and flared upward.

She felt stupid, as if she were still asleep. Were those men on horseback? In the flickering light one of the men turned his face toward her. Long black braids framed his face. His body was brown and he wore no shirt.

"Indians!" The word burst from her, "Indians!" she shouted again.

The three horsemen vanished into shadows and the sounds they made on the road soon died. Ellen had to stop and bend forward to quell the stitch in her side. "Am I dreaming?" she asked herself, then she ran again.

Behind her Uconthla and Conzey emerged from the kitchen doors. The sound of metal jangled against metal came faintly across the small distance. "They're bringing buckets," Ellen whispered toward the building as if to reassure the school house. She raced to the pump in back and tugged at the handle to press down, then she lifted the iron lever high.

"Come on!" she shouted to the pump. She strained to hasten the rhythm that would release water into the trough below the pump. A trickle, then a thin stream streamed into the stone receptacle in cadence with the up and down movement she made with the handle.

"Water's running," she shouted to Conzey who dropped the buckets he carried into the trough, scooped two buckets full and ran toward the front of the building. Uconthla was right behind him. She placed a blanket on Ellen's shoulders then scooped buckets full and ran around the building.

Water gushed full force into the tank and Ellen felt as if her body were welded to the heavy metal handle which she lifted and pushed down again and again.

Brown hands closed over hers and a voice spoke into her ear, "Go on, I'll pump now." Ellen stepped back and let Roman lift the water. Others with buckets raced to the trough. Soon a line formed from the pump to the front where the flames arched from the top of the door toward the roof of the building.

"Where did everyone come from?" Ellen asked, "I thought everyone was gone."

"The Hill," Roman answered. His face was hard and still in the dim light.

"The Hill?"

Roman didn't answer but bent to the pump with all his strength. His efforts kept the bucket brigade moving. It seemed only moments had passed when Ellen heard birds awakening and saw the sun rising over the school. She walked up the porch and through the charred front doorway behind Jake and Roman.

"It ain't too bad, Roman," Jake said.

Roman said nothing but he dug his boot heel into the blackness on the floor. "Just smoked a little. Floor seems stable." Jake smiled as he spoke. "Glad teacher was on the job."

Ellen felt tears rising. "We won't be able to open school."

Both men turned to her. They seemed surprised she was walking with them.

"Books are all right," Roman muttered as he turned back toward the classroom, "Books and desks."

"Weren't no accident," Jake frowned at the blackened doorway. "This here fire was set."

"Why did they do it?" Ellen asked "I saw them... three Indians. What caused them to...?"

"Indians?" Roman turned his questioning gaze on her.

"Three men. They had, at least one of them, had long braids and they weren't wearing shirts... they were brown...they..." her voice trailed off in the face of Roman's angry shout.

"Indians!" His hand exploded on a child's desk.

"Wasn't wearing shirts, you say?" Jake asked softly.

Ellen told them again of the long run toward the school and the three men on horseback in front of the building and how they'd disappeared on the road.

"I thought they were trying to help but they rode completely away," Ellen added.

"They wasn't putting it out, Missy, they was setting it, most likely." Jake said. He tuned with her to look at Roman at the front of the room. Ellen watched Roman trace across the letter on the backs of the Books of Knowledge.

"Some missing."

"Yes. I have them at home. Never mind that. What have I done to cause Indian men to want to burn up the school?"

"Now, little lady, nothing more can be done here right now." Jake stepped forward and took Ellen's arm. "You get right on back to the house and get yourself some rest. Me and Roman is going to look this place over." He moved her toward the opening where the front door had been. Roman also came toward her.

"I'll walk to the house with you."

Ellen shivered. She held her hand up toward Roman as if to ward him away. "Please... don't bother. I'll walk by myself... You..." She didn't finish her sentence but turned and ran alone through the early morning.

Chapter 9

Conzey tottered under the load of books he carried.

"Where?" he gasped.

"Dump them on the bed," Ellen ordered, "I'll arrange them on the shelves, thanks."

Uconthla stood in the dog run and peered into the bedroom. "Why bring all books from school?"

"We didn't bring all of them, just some of them."

"I fix."

Ellen moved to stop the older woman, "You go ahead with your work. I'll put these away."

Uconthla turned toward the kitchen, Conzey with her.

Ellen stepped out into the dog trot behind them.

"Conzey, you'd better spend your time helping clear away the burnt wood at the school house door."

When the old Indian turned without a word and started the walk toward the schoolhouse Ellen raised her hand to touch her lips. Oh, I'm Miss High and Mighty, getting used to ordering people around. She open her mouth to call Conzey back then stopped herself.

"He works here," she murmured, "Why shouldn't I tell him what to do?" She looked toward the other end of the dog trot. Unconthla stood just inside the darkened kitchen door.

She's watching me, Ellen thought. She raised her hand and waved to the older woman. Uconthla disappeared into the kitchen. Ellen shrugged and returned to her bedroom.

On the edge of the bed she sat leafing through each volume in the Book of Knowledge set. Soon she was printing words on a tablet. The message from Yahola began to take shape as she searched. Late in the afternoon she pushed her hair back from her face and sighed.

"I wish I had the 'R'," she said aloud. She looked at the last few lines she'd transcribed. "This is going so slowly."

Ellen softly mouthed Yahola's words, "You may need to get some help. Look to an advisor near you."

Before she could continue the work she heard the sound of boot heels on the wooden hallway.

"Jake," she called and followed the older man to the kitchen, "How did it go?"

"Not too bad, Missy. Me and Conzey got a lot of the worst cleared away. Gonna need a work party though." Jake accepted the tin cup of water Uconthla offered. He drank with small gulping sounds.

"A work party? How do we do that, Jake?"

"Me and Conzey'll get 'em to the school if'n you'll write the notes. Invite 'em for Friday. How about that?"

"I'll write them tonight."

"If'n you'll write some right now, me and Conzey can take 'em to quite a few folks afore sundown."

"Of course. I'll be just a little while." Ellen returned to her room. She tore off the page she'd been working on and pushed it into her small leather purse, then settled to writing invitations to meet at the Half Hollow Hill School for a "work party." By the time she had seven notes written, Jake knocked at the door.

"Oh, Jake, here." She thrust the papers into his hands. "I'll do more. Could you let Conzey do the rest of the delivering tomorrow?"

"I guess so. You need me for something?"

"I want to ride into Drumright and see Miss Grace Arnold." Ellen smiled an apology. "I'm afraid I wouldn't know how to get into town by myself."

"Why sure." Jake answered. "Conzey can do the invites and I'll take care of the new schoolmarm. You going to see the lawyer, huh?"

Ellen ignored his question. "Thanks Jake. Can we start early in the morning?"

"You bet."

It was a long time before Ellen slept. When she did she felt herself making the long run across the meadow toward the flaming building again. Again, the run seemed endless. She was surprised to see she did not run alone this time. A shadowy figure ran beside her, a figure with long black hair that streamed behind the runner. Ellen strained to see who raced beside her.

"Who are you?" she called.

"Hurry," was the answer she received, "Hurry. No time now. Hurry!"

Ellen awakened, her heart pounding.

"I think that was her." Ellen said aloud

Morning light seemed forever in coming but Ellen stayed huddled under the woven coverlet until she heard Jake's wagon moving up the lane.

Later, in the wagon with Jake, Ellen tried to explain the dream to him.

"No wonder you dreaming, girl. Fire is a scary thing."

"Oh Jake, I wasn't really dreaming of the fire. It was her. She was trying to tell me something, I think."

Jake pulled back on the reins and called "Whoa boys," then he turned on the wagon seat to look at Ellen.

"Now, dreams is dreams, Missy, and real is real. Better not get to mixing 'em up."

Ellen touched her purse, then opened it. The page of paper peeked from beneath her comb, mirror and tiny coin purse. She touched the corner of the paper with one finger then turned to stare at Jake as she silently repeated the message, "Look to an advisor near you." Probably not Jake, she decided.

In town, on the steps of the Fulkerson building, Ellen felt again for the paper. I'll tell the lawyer about this, she thought and she followed Jake's directions to the corner office that overlooked Drumright's main street.

Ellen pulled the message from her purse and handed it to the other woman. "This is the message, I've received. Does Yahola mean you?"

"I'm sorry, Miss Wiley," Grace Arnold moved to the office window. "You and Jake made that long trip in for nothing." She raised her hand to wave at the man seated in the wagon below, then turned to face Ellen. "I was Yahola's lawyer but I'm afraid she did not confide anything that would help us understand this message."

The lawyer raised the paper to the light from the window and read aloud. "Look to an advisor near you."

"You're a woman, you're educated, you're a lawyer."

"Yahola did trust me, Miss Wiley."

"Ellen."

"Ellen. But apparently she did not tell me everything. I managed her business affairs. That's all."

Ellen straightened at the lawyer's next whispered words, "Yahola was literal. If she said, 'near you' she meant physically near you, that would be my guess."

"But who?" Ellen felt frustration fill her. "I don't know who to turn to. What if I spoke to the person Yahola most feared?"

The lawyer placed her hand on Ellen's shoulder. "Let your heart guide you."

Ellen stirred from her reverie on the way home when Jake shouted, "Giddap," and leaned toward the team. Her right hand gripped the metal handhold and her left hand clutched her purse to her chest.

"What? Jake! What is it?"

Jake slapped the reins harder and spoke through gritted teeth.

"Bushwhackers!"

Ellen strained to see through the rising cloud of dust. "What?"

"Someone trying to ambush us, Missy."

Jake glanced to his left then back at the straining horses. "See off there... riding with us."

Ellen peered into the shadow of the trees. "Indians... they're Indians," she whispered.

The men and horses crowded toward the wagon. Jake redoubled his pleas for speed.

Ellen gasped, then added her own shouts to Jake's commands. "Hurry! They're closing in." Four men now pounded from the woods at Ellen's right. "More men, Jake. Look."

Jake didn't look to the right but he shouted to her. "I'm turning the team. You jump."

"But Jake..."

"Jump when I say."

"Jake..."

"Get ready..."

Jake suddenly pulled the horses into an open field to the left of the road.

"Jump!" he shouted.

The men pacing the wagon on the left bunched into a jumble of dust, rearing horses and shouted curses.

Ellen stood and dropped into the tall grass. Her legs felt driven into her body and she stumbled and rolled into the low brush. Her purse flew from her hand and she felt her dress catching and tearing as she slid to a stop. For a long moment she lay with her face in the dry undergrowth. She moved her arms, then her legs.

"I'm not broken," she whispered.

The shouts, the groans of the straining harness and the pounding of hooves seemed far away. For another second, Ellen lay face down then she pulled to her knees. She could see the horses of the bushwhackers closely surrounding Jake's still fast moving wagon.

"I've got to get out of here," she muttered and scrambled to her feet, then ducked to a squat. "Have to crawl," she moved slowly ignoring the pain where the brush and dried weeds cut into her hands and knees. As she moved she strained to hear the melee behind her. A moaning sobbing noise kept her from concentrating on the crashing noises on the road.

"What's happening?" she said aloud, "I can't hear," then she realized it was her own crying and moaning that kept the sounds from her. "Shut up!" she ordered herself.

The trees closed about her and Ellen pulled herself up the trunk of one of the black jacks. For a moment she stood embracing the small tree. The sounds became more and more distant. Ellen took a deep, shuddering breath and turned to move further into the woods.

She stepped into a narrow aisle between the trees, then stopped. In the treetops ahead, something glimmered.

"A light?" She stepped forward again, "Is that a light?" She moved another step toward the light. She felt drawn toward the shimmering sphere, in a moment she was almost running, the light moving ahead of her. When she slowed, the light slowed. When she was able to run, the light moved rapidly. She stumbled on a tree root and shouted, "Wait!" The light stopped instantly and moved back toward her.

"It's guiding me," Ellen mumbled, "It's helping me."

Time seemed suspended. Ellen couldn't judge whether a minute or an hour had passed. The light hovered at the edge of a clearing and Ellen felt a shock of recognition.

"That's Jake's lease house," She ran toward the structure, calling as she ran, "Mary, Mary."

Inside the cabin Mary listened to Ellen's incoherent story of the ambush. Mary made no comment but she reached for the shotgun and pulled Ellen toward the door.

"Come on."

The two women raced out the front door and down the road toward the place where Jake had turned off with their pursuers. When they'd run some distance down the side road Mary stopped Ellen with an upraised hand.

"Wait," the little woman whispered, "I see the wagon."

Ellen focused on the dark outline against the dusky sky, then she heard the movement of a horse. Both women stood unmoving while several seconds passed. The horse moved again and nickered softly in the dark.

"That there's one of our horses," Mary whispered, 'I think the bastards have killed my Jake and gone on."

"Yes. They've gone," Ellen echoed.

The two women advanced toward the wagon. A groan stopped them.

"Jake," Mary said aloud. She stepped quickly to the left and around the area where the wagon stood. "Jake, Jake," she called. The groan sounded again and Mary broke into a run then she knelt beside the man. His head was only inches from the front hooves of the team.

"Hold the horses," Mary shouted.

Ellen slipped into the space between the animals and took a guide rein in each hand. "Is Jake all right?"

"I think so. He's warm and he's breathing. Honey, can you talk?"

"Yeah," Jake's voice was low. "I ain't dead yet."

"Can you get up? Ellen'll hold the horses and I'll help you into the wagon. I want to get you home."

Ellen stared at the road stretching before her. She held the reins in one hand. "Are they coming back?" she asked aloud, "There's a light."

Jake steadied himself by pulling himself up on the edge of the wagon. Mary moved under his arm and urged him to lean on her shoulders. All three stood immobile as the light moved to a place above their heads. Time seemed to stop and the air shimmered with a sound that was also a light.

With the radiance around them Ellen could see her purse lying in the road ahead of them, objects from the purse scattered here and there, some off into the grass.

Still no one moved.

Jake laughed, then coughed. "Lookie there," he rasped and pointed upward. Ellen looked up to where he pointed.

"Who is it?" she whispered.

"Just a reminder little lady." Jake smiled down at his wife. "Mary ain't it just like I told you? It pays to carry some of that there Indian blood mixed in with that there white eye stuff, don't it?" He laughed again.

Chapter 10

Ellen looked at the crowded desks then at the men standing against the walls of the room. Voices were loud and snatches of conversation pounded against her ears.

"Damned Indians..."

"Fixico better have something to start..."

"Well, Mary done said..."

Ellen turned toward a rustling disturbance at the front. Roman Fixico stepped to the corner of the teacher's desk. His eyes moved to take in the crowd. It looked as if he studied each individual, Ellen thought. He removed the pale Stetson and placed it on the desk beside him. Then, his gaze locked with Ellen's and she felt as though she was being held in his dark liquid stare. His didn't waver and Ellen broke the stare first. She looked at the floor then back at the huge Indian. His gaze remained on hers.

Again Ellen looked away.

Why does he stare at me? She asked herself inwardly.

The voices soon quieted and the men and women began to concentrate on the silent Indian. Roman surveyed them but still didn't speak.

Ellen felt anger rising. Why doesn't he say something? she asked herself, He's the one who called this meeting.

As if he could hear her thought, the dark gaze again locked with her own. Ellen felt a small jolt in her chest. Am I afraid of him? She questioned herself, Is that why he makes me feel so strange?

When Roman finally spoke, it was not about the ambush nor about accusations being leveled at the Indians. He spoke of the need for cleaning and repairing the damage to the schoolroom.

As he continued to speak other people in the room called out ideas for planning work to be done. Ellen felt herself staring at the Indian man on the teacher's platform. For long moments she sat unblinking, staring at the gleam of lamplight as it reflected on his satiny skin.

The voices dropped and moved outside her consciousness. The only reality was the dark eyes, the gleaming skin, the shining black hair. It was as though she were trapped within the aura of his male beauty.

She heard her name and struggled to respond. Her anger returned. He was talking with her, disturbing her dream.

"Miss Wiley," his voice was soft, a caress across the crowded room. "Would you like to say something?"

Ellen felt color rising in her cheeks. "Whatever is decided will be fine."

"We cannot decide without our teacher's suggestions." His smile seemed to mock her. She opened her mouth to say something hard, something to turn his eyes away from her. He's laughing at me, she thought as she glimpsed the amusement in his eyes. Again she tried to form a word.

From the blackened doorway a loud male voice interrupted.

"Now, ain't this something? I guess nobody thought to tell me they was a meeting here tonight."

"Come in Mr. Caudill. You are welcome." Roman's voice was quiet but a cold heaviness weighted his words. "Join us in our discussions."

"Yeah, I'll do that." The driller moved into the light. His eyes roved over the crowd and stopped at Ellen. "Move over Miss Schoolmarm. I'll just share that desk there with you."

Ellen flushed again but moved to make room on the child sized double bench to make room for the oil man. She felt a fierce joy fill her. Blood pounded in her temples. That will show him, she said within herself. For a moment her thoughts faltered. Show him what? she wondered but the exultation returned. I don't need an Indian, certainly not Mr. Grand and Wonderful Fixico. She slid over slightly as Merle Caudill slipped behind the double desk with her.

She smiled at the driller and from beneath her lashes she looked again at the young man in the front of the room, but Roman Fixico was not attending to her any longer. He was already involved with offers to repair, to clean, to renew. He didn't look in her direction again.

Ellen felt dull emptiness rising within her.

"I don't care," she whispered to herself.

"What say? I need to talk to you," the driller's words cut across her thoughts. Ellen put a finger across her lips to silence him but she nodded.

Why not? she asked herself, and she turned on the bench to smile at the oil man. He returned the smile and Ellen pulled her attention back to the talk around her. Why doesn't the man shut up? she asked herself. She listened to Roman's words, stoking her own private anger. He sounds so...so...so...Indian, but her gaze was again drawn to the dark face.

Roman smiled at an offer to help re-shingle the front wall area, and Ellen felt so drawn to the sudden glimpse of straight white teeth glistening against the deep bronze of his skin, that she shivered.

Her friends in St. Louis would much prefer Merle Caudill. She knew that quite well. Falling in love with an Indian was out of the question!

Chapter 11

Ellen turned away from the wardrobe to find Uconthla staring at her from the open door.

"Did you want something, Uconthla? I'll be dressed and ready for breakfast in just a moment."

"Man come for you."

"Man come for me... what does that mean?" Ellen pulled the peach colored voile dress down about her hips then struggled to reach the catch at the back of the neck.

"I fix." The Indian woman moved to stand behind Ellen.

"Thanks. Now, what did you say?"

Uconthla lifted the ruffle of peach voile and let it float back into place at the neckline. She fluffed the gauzy bow at the hip of the dress then lifted the circular skirt to reveal flesh colored silk hose rolled above Ellen's knee.

"Pretty. Good you dress up, wear silk hose."

"Uconthla, I'm just dressing for breakfast, then some work at the school... but I'm glad you like the dress. Of course the hose were your idea."

The older woman leaned close to the younger. Her mouth barely moved. "Indian man like pretty clothes. You go with him." Uconthla nodded her head with some secret satisfaction. "You go."

Ellen raised her voice. "Uconthla! Tell me at once what you're talking about."

Uconthla smiled and turned toward the door. She left the bedroom without another word.

Ellen stared after her for a moment, then shrugged and turned back to the mirror. "Crazy," she murmured.

The sound of horse's hooves pulled her away from the dressing table. She turned then placed the brush atop the wardrobe without making a sound as she edged toward the window. She looked out at Roman Fixico who looked solemnly back in at her. "Good morning, teacher." He lifted his hat and nodded.

"What are you doing right outside my bedroom window?"

The corner of the Indian's mouth lifted slightly. "When I sit on Tiger that puts me just even with the lower pane of your window ma'am."

"I can see that. What I want to know is why you are here at all. I mean, why is your horse standing outside my window so you and Tiger are just even with the window opening?"

Again the tiny smile. "I do not know why Tiger chose to stand just below your window, teacher, but he did and I am on his back. I am lucky, am I not?"

"Maybe not so lucky if you don't tell me right now what you want!"

Roman's smile grew and Tiger sidestepped nearer the window.

Ellen touched the peach colored ruffle at her neckline. The man on the horse intently studied the gesture then nodded as if agreeing with something unspoken.

After a long moment he whispered, "Today you will go to the house of the Fixico family. We have prepared food for you."

Ellen felt shock radiating through her. That's what Uconthla was talking about. *Somehow she knew Roman Fixico was going to invite me to his house today.* She shivered and felt the hair at the back of her neck prickle then she shrugged the fear away. Of course, she explained to herself, he told her he was coming here. *That's why she put out my silk stockings.* She stood silently for another moment then she smiled at the waiting man.

"Uconthla told me to go, so of course I must go" She moved a step back. "I will be ready in a few minutes. Shall I change to riding clothes?"

Roman looked at her with great interest. "I like what you are wearing. Conzey is hitching the buggy for us. I will let Tiger make the trip home by himself."

In the buggy Ellen tried once again to learn how Uconthla had known of Roman's coming. "I suppose you told Uconthla you were coming for me?" She tried to keep her voice light. He turned his gaze toward her but said nothing but shook his head "no" then turned his gaze toward the road.

Ellen insisted. "Uconthla knew you were coming for me."

"Uconthla is one of the old ones."

"What does that mean?"

"It means she knows things."

The road widened and the pin oaks circled a small meadow. Flame colored flowers danced in the sunlight. Ellen felt breathless with the beauty of the day and the place. She touched Roman's silk sleeve. "Do stop for a moment. This is so lovely."

He obediently slowed the buggy then stopped it. With wheels and hooves stilled Ellen could hear birds. After a second an insect started again on his interrupted song.

"What are they?" Ellen indicated the flowers that seemed to have been planted in small patches throughout the open space.

"White men call them 'Indian Paint Brush'." Roman answered. "I do not know the scientific name for them. And yes, they are one of the lovely things about Oklahoma."

Ellen closed her eyes and murmured, "I love Oklahoma."

Roman remained silent but Ellen felt his finger trace a symbol on the back of her hand. She opened her eyes but did not look at him. Again, he drew the sign on her left hand. She watched the brown hand move above her white one.

"What is it?" she whispered.

"It is our family sign. I am preparing you."

"Preparing me?"

"To be with; no, not with, *in* the family."

I should be indignant, Ellen thought, angry at his touch, but she didn't move, didn't speak as the brown hand drew the symbol once again upon her own. Again she closed her eyes. I could swim in this sunshine, she thought when she felt the buggy begin to move more slowly than before. I never knew sunlight could be heavy, like a liquid. When the buggy stopped again Ellen opened her eyes with reluctance.

"The heat is making me sleepy," she said aloud and she felt no surprise when she looked to the side of the road and saw a young woman standing in the sun. Light glinted from the woman's long black hair.

"Who is she, Roman?" Ellen gestured toward the young woman. The chill returned at his answer which was a question.

"Do you not recognize your cousin, Yahola? She gives us her benediction."

Ellen stared at the young Indian woman. Yahola smiled and Ellen was surprised to feel herself smiling in return. Roman clucked at the horse and again the buggy moved forward. Yahola stood a moment without moving then she turned and glided toward the trees. Ellen watched the young woman disappear into the woods.

"She's gone. Was that really Yahola?"

"It is said that she returns." Roman slowed the horse then he pointed through the trees. "Our house," he whispered. Ellen could see patches of white through the mass of dark trunks.

"Not a log cabin," she spoke aloud. The surprise pulled her fully back into the moment.

"Not a log cabin," Roman agreed and he covered a smile with one hand. "Not even a tepee." The white frame structure stood in the center of a well swept yard. Out buildings snuggled under the trees some distance from the main house. Ellen silently counted the floors.

"Three floors?" Again she spoke aloud.

Again Roman agreed with her, "Indeed. Three floors."

"It's huge." Ellen's stare was riveted to the steeply pitched dormers near the shingled roof. "Maybe four floors."

"It serves us well," Roman commented.

Ellen realized her mouth was open with astonishment. She pulled her gaze to the man who watched her with seeming amusement.

"It's bigger than Half Hollow Hill," Her tone was accusing.

At this, Roman laughed aloud. "Your reactions to my home have been quite interesting," he said, "Can you tell me what you were expecting?"

Ellen smiled then, also. "Well, it is much further back in the woods. How was I to know it would be the grandest place in Oklahoma?"

"Not the grandest," the young man leaned to stop the horse, "But large enough for a big family. My father built it."

"Who built my house?"

"My uncle, who was also Yahola's grandfather, built the Half Hollow place." His tone softened, "Your house is very special to all of us." He jumped from the buggy, handed the reins to a boy who appeared from behind a large forsythia bush.

"Who is he?" Ellen asked.

"A small cousin," Roman answered. "Soon you will meet them all." He reached to help Ellen to the ground, "Get ready to hear much Creek spoken. Some of the aunties don't speak English."

"Tell me something about your tribe."

"We call ourselves 'Muskogee.' The British white eyes called us 'Creeks' because we liked to live near rivers." Roman took her hand in his.

Ellen flushed warm at his touch. She looked up into the brown eyes, then toward the enormous house. No one was visible at any window nor on the wide verandah that surrounded two sides of the house.

For a moment both stood looking up at the house.

"Did Yahola come here?"

"Often when we were children. Not so often when we were grown. She came here last with your friend, the oil man."

"Merle Caudill?"

"Yes."

They stepped onto the wide porch. The front door stood open but all was quiet.

"You will see some differences in the way we live," Roman explained, "We do not come shouting to the yard when visitors arrive. We wait until they come inside before we greet them." He mused a moment, "And not all who come here are invited in."

Ellen's eyes looked a question.

"Ah, yes. You, Miss School Teacher... you are our honored guest today. Come inside."

Ellen stepped into a square entry hall. Stairs rose to the right of the hall. The hall and the stair were empty of furnishings or carpeting.

"We do not clutter our lives or our houses with unnecessary things," Roman gestured toward an open doorway to Ellen's left, "In there many await you."

Ellen stepped into a large room. Her confused impression was of dark faces looking at her from every side. She could hear Roman speaking and she heard the word, "Yahola" repeated by the people there.

Some of the people sat in wooden or wicker chairs, some sat on the polished floor. Above the mantle at the back of the room was a bookshelf which extended to the ceiling. Some objects that Ellen could not identify were placed here and there on the shelves but on the topmost shelf was a familiar green-backed book.

Ellen shivered. "R" she said to herself. "The R volume."

She looked at Roman but he was involved in a low voiced discussion with a listening circle of people. Ellen tried to read their impassive faces. They're talking about me, she thought. I know that because they're trying so hard not to look at me.

From beneath lowered lashes she peered at the groups about the room. All eyes were turned away from her. She wrapped both arms across her chest. Cool in here, she thought.

Three of the women near Roman slipped from the room and returned carrying platters.

"Fry Bread," Roman murmured, "Our Creek delicacy. You will try it."

Ellen looked at the golden brown crescents. The smiling aunts offered the food, holding platters toward her. None of the three looked Ellen in the eye.

"No forks," again Roman murmured words close to Ellen's ear. He lifted a piece of the bread to his mouth, touched it lightly with his lips then handed it to Ellen. "I promise... you will like it." His eyes laughed into hers. As if he read her thoughts Roman said, "We use the same raw ingredients the 'White eyes' use. We just make the food better! Try something."

Ellen bit into the warm bread. "You're right," she felt surprise enter her voice. "This is delicious." Why did he kiss the bread, she wondered, or was that a kiss?

The visit passed in a whirl of strange dark faces, strange foods and unknown words. Ellen began to feel as if she were divided. Part of her nodded, ate and listened as the household's activities swirled about her. Part of her seemed to hover overhead to watch the Ellen below as she smiled and talked and moved about.

The Ellen who ate and talked with the Indian Aunts turned in concert with the Ellen who observed from above. The two Ellens realized that Jake Linder was standing in the doorway of the room. With a sharp jolt the two seemed to come together into one Ellen again. At that moment, standing at floor level, everything in the room came more sharply into focus.

"Jake," Ellen's voice sounded loud in her own ears, "What are you doing here?"

"Thought I'd come and ride along home with you, ma'am."

"Roman... uh, Mr. Fixico brought me here in the buggy from Half Hollow Hill."

"I know, ma'am. I'll just ride along with you two." Jake looked at the polished floor in front of him as he spoke again. "Lessen you was to have some objections."

Ellen looked at Roman. His face was impassive. At a subtle signal from him, one of the women walked to Jake and offered a platter of food.

Jake lifted a piece of Fry Bread toward Roman. "Thanks pardner."

"We're about ready to leave, Jake," the Indian motioned at Ellen and walked toward the front hall, "We shall go by the caves."

Ellen's hand covered her mouth, then as quickly fell to her side. "The caves?"

"Now, Roman, I don't know about trying that there..."

"We will ride to Half Hollow Hill," Roman's voice overrode Jake's words.

"I can't wait to see the caves," she whispered. Excitement filled her chest.

"I will ride Tiger while you see to the school teacher's buggy," Roman strode from the room before Ellen could say another word.

"I guess I'm riding with you, Jake." Ellen grinned because the thrill of exploration was about to be hers. The ride to the caves took only a few minutes. Ellen felt disoriented, as if something more were necessary, as if the journey had ended too suddenly. She looked ahead to the edge of the cliff in front of them, then back at the almost invisible trail which the three of them had just followed.

"I thought you lived a long way from Half Hollow Hill." Her statement held accusation. "It took us hours to get to your place this morning. Now, we are in back of my house in a matter of minutes."

"Yes, you can come to my house very quickly," Roman explained, "But you cannot come in a car and usually not in a buggy. The driver must be very familiar with the trail since the public road takes a roundabout way to explode upon my family." Roman smiled the smile that did not reach his eyes. "The Fixicos prefer it that way."

"Not many folks want to cross the sacred ground... leastwise, not at night." Jake explained, "And that's the onliest way to Fixico's place from Half Hollow." He strode to check the horse's bit and bridle. "Lessen you was to use the road."

"Roads are for white men," Roman said, "We only use the road when we pretend to be white-eyes."

Ellen felt as if a heavy veil were just beginning to lift. *Now I know how the Indians can be at the schoolhouse in minutes... and how they can just appear or disappear. Half Hollow and the Fixico farm are practically back to back.*

She stood at the edge of the sandstone cliff and looked out over her cabin and the schoolhouse in the distance. She could see the dark fire line at the front of the schoolhouse roof. She turned to ask Roman about the roof. He and Jake were working with the buggy and the horse. She turned back to look at the clearing where her house sat. *The road... she thought, and the Indians... the men who set the fire... went...to the road... heading...*she looked at the road again and nodded before she finished her thought*... toward the town... toward Drumright.*

She stepped toward the two men. "The Indians," she stopped then began again, more loudly this time, "They didn't come this way."

"What's that, Missy?" Jake joined her at the edge of the cliff.

Ellen looked past the older man. "Where's Roman going?"

"Letting the horses drink. You was saying...?"

"Jake, do all the Indians in the area live back up this way?"

Jake nodded and pointed toward the clearing below. "Half Hollow Hill lies out in the front of all the Indian's places. I reckon Yahola was the one Indian that lived closest to Drumright. Now it's you."

Ellen stared at Jake. "Me!"

"Yeah. Far as I know you're the closest Indian to the whites. All the rest back in here for a good many miles is Indian. Mostly Creek."

Ellen whirled toward Jake. She pointed toward her own face. "Jake," She lightly touched her own nose with her finger, "Look. Look at me. Do you see an Indian standing here?" Ellen was smiling but Jake returned her look of amusement with a perplexed frown.

"You are now, ain't you?"

"Jake, don't be silly. You're scaring me. I'm Ellen. Old white-eyes-from-Missouri-Ellen. What does that mean, 'I am now?'"

"Well, you was to the Fixico's today and all, and they come up to meet you and Roman was saying..." Jake's voice trailed away. He shook his head and turned to leave. "I'll go see if'n Roman needs some help."

Ellen felt astonishment rising through every part of her body. "You think I have somehow become an Indian?" But she was speaking to Jake's back as he disappeared into the brush.

Forget that nonsense, Ellen commanded herself. You're up here at last, at the caves. She peered downward through the rocks. I can see the cave openings... some of them. She looked for a way to move down onto the entry ledge. Before she found a way down, Roman emerged from the trees behind her, Jake followed in the buggy.

"Come on Missy," Jake called, "We better be getting you on home."

"But I haven't seen the caves. My caves."

Roman danced Tiger toward her. "Someday very soon, you and I will come here, Miss Schoolteacher," He leaned to extend a hand to her. "You go with Jake now and I will prepare the old ones for you."

Ellen pulled her hand from his. "Are these or aren't these caves a part of my property?"

"By the white man's measure, yes, but the caves are not yet ready for you... or perhaps you are not yet ready for them." Roman smiled and touched the brim of his hat. "Soon you will visit your caves and I will be with you."

Jake called again. "We're going to have to go back by the road, little lady. Take us some time. Better come on."

In the buggy, Ellen held her questions until they reached the level ground. "Jake what did you mean?"

"What's that?"

"When you said I was an Indian."

Jake's smile was uneasy. "I guess I was speaking out of turn, Miss," He clucked to the horse. "Talking about something I don't know nothing about."

"You were serious. You thought I had somehow become an Indian."

Jake pointed with his whip. "Half Hollow Hill is right close."

Ellen sagged against the back of the buggy seat. "Well, I guess that's one of the things you don't want to talk about now. One of the many things." Her voice gained volume. "And another thing, Jake. I think those Indians that set the fire were..."

Jake forced the horse into a run and raced into the schoolyard. He shouted to stop the animal then turned toward Ellen. His voice was loud in the sudden quiet.

"You, Miss Ellen. If'n I was you I'd put Indians and Indian doings right out of my head." He jumped to the ground and moved to her side. "Here now, I'll help you down and you can go do that work you was complaining about not doing. I'll just take this rig on up to the house."

Before Ellen could say more than, "But Jake, I think I know..." the buggy was moving, leaving her standing in the sandy track.

Chapter 12

Inside the classroom Ellen spread the books before her. I like working here, she thought, this classroom is mine. Why does it seem so much *more* mine?

Uconthla slipped into the room. For a moment she said nothing then she motioned to Ellen. "You come." Her words were low. "Oilman at house. You come."

"Merle Caudill? At the house?"

"You come. Be careful." Uconthla's voice carried a sense of urgency. "Watch out for roughneck oilman."

On the walk home Uconthla spoke no more but Ellen could hear the Indian woman give an occasional grunt or snort. Once Ellen thought she heard the word, "Oilman."

Caudill stood at the dogtrot watching the two of them approach. When they neared the house, Ellen stopped and waited for the visitor to step down from the porch.

"I come to invite you over to our rig."

Ellen glanced back at Uconthla but the woman had already moved toward the kitchen.

"Why not?" Ellen recalled the hours with Roman and his family. "I've fooled away most of the day. Let's make it a complete vacation."

As they walked away, Ellen could hear Conzey chanting strange words. Once in awhile Uconthla's voice would add something.

"Uconthla's saying my name," Ellen said.

"Mine too," Merle laughed. "Crazy as coots, both of 'em."

Before they were out of earshot Ellen heard Yohola's name added to the song that wasn't a melody. For a long time she could hear the voices rise and fall in strange cadences.

"I've been meaning to visit your drilling site." Ellen spoke when the chanting could no longer be heard.

"And I been meaning to come and get you to visit."

"Your rig is really very close to my house when we walk, isn't it?" She surveyed the hillside above them.

"Yeah, road takes longer."

Ellen pointed. "I've been wanting to go up to the caves."

The oilman stopped. "Well, we could go there now. That's one of the things I wanted to talk over." He faced the line of hills. "You really oughta let us do some exploratory work up there."

"What would that be?"

"You oughta let us put a rig up there on your property. See if you got oil." Caudill patted Ellen on the shoulder. "I got a feeling you could get to be one rich little lady." He smiled and turned back to view the caves. "Must be plenty oil up there."

"Do you really think so?"

"I know so, little lady."

"Why haven't you or someone drilled up there already?"

"Crazy Indians," he muttered.

Ellen was shocked at the indignation that rose within her. *He had no right to call them crazy.* Then she remembered she'd called them that herself, plenty of times.

Merle had to ask his question twice to get her attention. "Want to climb up there? Now?"

Ellen nodded but stayed rooted to the spot. "I'm wearing my silk stockings." Her feet seemed reluctant to start the climb to the nearest cave.

"Aw, come on." His voice penetrated her confusion. "Ain't nothing going to ruin your stockings. If they run I'll get you a new pair."

Roman said not to go. The inner warning came as if spoken in her ear. She stepped toward the trail that led upward, then stopped. Again Merle's voice challenged her.

"Come on, Schoolmarm. I been meaning to look them caves over."

"You're catching the craziness," she said aloud.

"What'd you say?"

"Wait for me."

Outside the first cave Ellen seated herself on the sun warmed boulder that jutted over the flat area below.

"Good exercise."

"Yes," she agreed. "Good exercise. A truly beautiful place. It's wonderful seeing my house and the school from this high up." In the silence the chanting from Uconthla Goat and Conzey Bucktrot drifted up to where Ellen sat. "I feel like I'm dreaming," Ellen said. "Nothing seems real."

"Real enough." Ellen heard the oilman's answer. He reached for her hand and pulled her up to finish the climb. He stepped close to her and looked down into her eyes.

Ellen found the pale blue gaze disturbing, but she could not turn away. In a moment the oilman broke the tension with one word.

"Sometime." He moved an inch closer. "Sometime." Then he turned and helped Ellen up the rocky pathway.

Relief filled Ellen. She asked herself what she would do when the "sometime" came.

At the first cave opening Merle turned. "Ready?"

Ellen's movements became even more hesitant. "Mr. Caudill... Merle...maybe... I shouldn't go in." The words Roman had spoken earlier in the day repeated in her mind. *The caves are not ready for you, Ellen.*

"Well, why not? We climbed a long way." His hand tightened on hers. "You ain't going to back out now, are you, little lady?"

Ellen raised her chin. After all, she thought, these caves belong to me. I *should* see them. She placed her right foot on the shadow just inside the entrance."

Merle tugged again. "Come on. I want to see the configuration here."

"Configuration?"

"Yeah. These caves and this whole hill looks good for drilling."

Several steps into the opening the passageway seemed to push up and outward. "It's huge," Ellen whispered.

"No need to whisper," the oilman's voice was a raucous intrusion in the cool quiet of the wide stone room. A deeper darkness revealed another passageway opening at the back of the first area.

"It's bigger than I thought," Again Ellen whispered. She felt a prickling on the outside of her arms and legs. A heavy feeling, half excitement, half dread, lay somewhere within her chest. Merle's voice echoed from a distance.

"Hey, let's go on back there. I want to see the rest of this."

Cold air washed across her ruffled neckline and the fabric rose and fell in a swift movement, as if someone had flicked the pale cloth from left to right.

Ellen wanted to ask the oilman to come back but her mouth found no words. She could see him entering the second passageway, gesturing to her. Unseen hands pushed her toward him but she could not say anything. In the darkness of the passage, behind Caudill, Ellen could see the reflection of a fire, a campfire. The even larger cavern that opened before them seemed filled with a glow that leaped to the roof of the cavern then fell back to a communal fire. Figures moved in front of the golden light. Ellen glimpsed feathers and a wide brimmed hat. On one head sat the crown of a buffalo head with the two stubby horns protruding upward.

Again the chilly wind whipped the peach colored voile and caused the circular skirt to whirl and lift against Ellen's body. Her voice seemed to lift and whirl as well. "What's going on?"

"What say?"

The face of the oilman turned toward her. His smile was twisted white in the orange of his face. His eyes seemed empty black sockets, his hair glowed a greenish yellow in the strange light.

Ellen stepped backward until the walls of the passageway pressed into her shoulders.

"Merle." Her voice rasped with the effort to speak. "Who are they?"

The death's head leered at her again. "What're you talking about, little lady?"

"I can see through them," she whispered then she repeated the words, this time in a scream that echoed against the stone walls. "I can see *through* them!"

Chapter 13

The walk down to the house seemed to be happening to someone else. Ellen heard Merle's words as he helped her from rock to rock but her mind remained on the dancing figures in the cave.

"I could see through them," she murmured.

The oilman stopped and looked back up at her. She saw the line across his face where his hat shaded him from sunburn. In the light of the late afternoon Merle Caudill looked normal, just an ordinary, good looking American working man.

Why was I afraid of him? She wondered. Merle's lips moved and Ellen forced herself to listen and try to respond.

"You been out in the sun too long today, little lady." He smiled and they moved on down. "Can't trifle with this Oklahoma sun." She took the last step onto the level path at the back of her house. "What you need is a change of scene."

Ellen hastened her pace. My room, she thought. I have to get to my room and try to reason out what happened. But the oilman clung to Ellen's hand. "What is it Merle? I need to go in."

"Couple of things. I want you to come over to the rig tomorrow. I'll show you what a good crew I got."

"What else?" She felt as though she were being physically pulled toward the house but the driller held her hand and waited for her to turn back to him.

"Got me a car."

"A car!"

"Thought you might want to ride along." He smiled again. "You ever ride in a car, little lady?"

Ellen shook her head.

"Well? Want to go? Want to ride with me?"

Ellen nodded then returned his smile. "I've never ridden in a car. I didn't know you knew how to drive an automobile, Merle. I'd love to go. Thank you."

"Yeah, I know a lot of things about machinery." He strutted closer. "I'll pick you up in the morning. We'll stop by the rig then drive on into Drumright. You might feel like a little shopping, huh?"

Ellen glanced at her worn white slippers. "I need some walking shoes... or maybe boots."

"You can get 'em tomorrow."

"Thanks Merle." She stepped up to the kitchen door. "I'll be waiting for you." She waved then moved on into the dim room. "Uconthla," she called.

The old woman's voice rose from the space beside the wood stove. "You go caves. You see."

"What?"

"You see ancestors."

The dancing figures flooded back into Ellen's mind. "Oh, let's not talk about that." She moved on toward her bedroom. As she entered the chamber she slammed the door behind her but she still heard the chant from the kitchen.

"Old ones come too soon. Too soon. Too soon."

"Shut up!" Ellen's shout silenced the old woman but the last words the Indian woman had spoken seemed to reverberate in the wooden hall. "Too soon. Too soon. Too soon."

Ellen backed into her room until she felt the bedframe touch her legs. She sat down. "I'm going crazy." She spoke aloud and her eyes widened. "Crazy. I've been seeing things."

Ellen's hand shook as it moved to touch her mouth. Her fingers covered the opening to smother the word "crazy" but she heard the sound repeat inside herself. *Crazy.*

Dressing for bed took a long time. Several times Ellen found herself standing unmoving, staring into space. Finally she shook herself back to reality by examining her silk hose. Perfect condition. She tossed them onto a chair. I'm not crazy. How could Uconthla know what I saw? She slipped a cotton gown over her shoulders. That was some kind of trick up there.

After she blew out the lamp, Ellen lay awake as the silvered moonlit rectangle moved across the floor of her room. The only sound she heard was the muffled thud from the cable tool rig.

"Sounds like drums," she whispered, "Like Indian drums." She closed her eyes and the beat of the drilling tool became a part of her dream.

Chapter 14

"We're bouncing across ruts at twenty miles an hour," Merle shouted, "How do you like that?"

Ellen smiled and waited for a smooth stretch before she answered.

"Are we really going twenty miles an hour?"

"She'll do 50."

Ellen looked at the pressure gauge at the very front of the black hood. None of the girls in St. Louis would believe it. I had to come to the wilds of Oklahoma to get a ride in a Model T. She glanced at Merle's profile. And with a good-looking driver, too. She allowed a tiny smile.

Merle slowed the car when he turned into the deeply rutted trail that led to the drilling site.

"We'll have to walk part way."

"I don't mind. I can see things better when I'm walking. I have just learned that a car moves too fast. You miss things."

Merle pulled the brake on and let the engine die.

"So quiet," Ellen said, "I can't hear anything except the... the..." her voice trailed off, "Except the pounding of the rig." She finished the thought inside herself, like last night, only louder.

As they moved nearer the rig the thumping stopped. Ellen looked a question at Merle but he hurried on ahead of her.

A swarm of overalled men clustered in the center of the wooden derrick floor. Merle moved to join the men. She watched him and the men from the edge of the clearing. The men pulled and hauled on the heavy equipment at the center of the floor, then they all scattered to other parts of the rig and the pounding began once more. Moments later Merle was back at her side. He gestured for Ellen to follow him.

Close to the rig a small tin building stood on the path.

"What's this little house for? Does someone live here?"

"We call it the doghouse. Most rigs have one. The men use it to change, or rest... or eat in when the weather's bad. Come on. I'll introduce you to them old boys." Merle leaped to the floor of the rig, then turned and pulled Ellen up to the wooden platform.

Ellen nodded and smiled at the shouted introductions. The names were drowned in the thud and clink of the cable tools.

She heard one of the men shout, "School Teacher?" then she watched Merle nod. Merle grinned when a second man shouted, "Got yourself another schoolmarm?"

Merle's answer to the man was low.

"What did that man mean, another teacher?"

"Guess he was talking about Yahola. She come here a couple of times."

He looked up quickly and Ellen knew he could read the surprise on her face. Yahola? Here at his rig? Why? The Indians were so dead set against this drilling activity, weren't they? Ellen felt the shock of memory this time.

"Yahola was here. Up there." Ellen pointed to the wooden platform high overhead, "Up there... I saw her up there the day I came to Half Hollow Hill. I saw her from the wagon. The wind was blowing her hair."

"Ain't been no woman on this here rig for some time." Merle answered. "You been seeing things. Anyway, Yahola's been dead nigh onto a year now."

Ellen felt another shock tremble through her.

Merle turned away at a shout from one of his crew.

"Be with you in a second," he shouted. He turned back to her. "Got to go help pull that thing. We're a man short today."

When the oil man had joined his crew Ellen heard the men's curses and laughter. He gaze wandered up again to the smaller platform high above them. An anchor cable went from atop the rig out to somewhere in the woods. Precaution against the wind, she thought.

"The monkey board," she whispered, "Yahola..." She stepped back to try to see the wooden platform a bit better. She jumped when she felt a hand on her arm.

"Want to climb up there?"

"Oh, I couldn't."

"Come on. I'll go up with you. Safe as churches."

"It's so high."

"Good view. Come on, kiddo. We'll go take a look then we'll go on in to Drumright." Merle pushed a short ladder to the bottom of the set of cross bars which were nailed onto the wooden rig.

Again, Ellen felt the pull toward the ladder. She stepped forward two steps, then stopped.

"You go first, hon," Merle urged.

Ellen stepped forward one more step. "It's so high." She stopped again.

"Go on."

"I want to... but I'm scared." She moved again. Her fingers brushed the wood. Warm, she thought, feels alive. The wood vibrated under her palm. She looked at Merle. "That cable doesn't help. The whole rig is moving."

Merle grinned and gestured with his thumb. He shouted. "Everything in the oil business moves, little lady. Go on up."

Ellen put her foot on the first rung. Her body trembled. *I'm really going to climb up there. Up there where I saw Yahola that first day.*

She looked back toward the men gathered around the cable tool drill hole. No one was working. Their faces were turned toward her. No one smiled. No one spoke.

"What's wrong? Why are they looking at us?'

Merle gestured upward again with his thumb. "Go on. They think a woman on a rig is bad luck. Superstitious."

Ellen pulled herself from the ladder to the cross bars. For a second she hesitated. She looked again at the workers. For another moment she paused then began to climb steadily.

Near the opening to the monkey board she felt a compulsion to look down. Merle's head bobbed upward toward her.

I could jam my foot on his head and knock him to the ground below, she thought. Horror spread through her as she realized what she had just contemplated. "What's wrong with me?" She mouthed the words.

She scrambled up the last few rungs and through the opening onto the smaller wooden platform. She pulled herself to her knees then stood upright. She stared down through the opening where the brown felt hat moved toward her with each step the oilman took.

Ellen felt her hair flutter in the wind.

Something soft moved across her face and smoothed her hair back. Warmth moved against the nape of her neck. She raised both arms and it was as if a reassuring touch moved across the fingers of each hand. Something pressed against her to cause her to step away from the opening and turn toward the railing.

"I can see the house, the school," she gasped. "The caves. I can see everything."

"Yeah," the oil man's voice was just behind her. "I got to admit that sometimes I watch you."

"From up here?"

"Yeah. Keep track of you that way." He laughed. "It's always a real pretty sight."

Ellen moved her attention to the hill and the caves behind the house. Another gasp escaped her. They were there... the dancers... the Indians... at the mouth of the cave.

She pointed toward the caves and whispered, "Look!" As the exclamation left her mouth the figures disappeared. Ellen blinked.

"I saw the dancers again," she said, "The dancers from the cave." She shivered and again felt the warm touch on her arm. She looked at Merle to see if he felt it also.

"Women's imaginings," He laughed and put an arm about her shoulders. "You been listening to them Indians. Damn heathens." He looked down into Ellen's face. "Easy to believe all that stuff if you fool around with them folks."

With his chin he pointed in the way to the Fixico ranch.

"I saw you coming from Fixico's spread. That ain't no place for a white woman, little lady. Bunch of squaws and bucks back in there. And that there Roman," His arm tightened about her. "You'd best stay down there at home where you belong. Down at Half Hollow Hill."

Ellen closed her eyes. A sinking feeling held her motionless within the oil man's grasp. Half Hollow Hill can be looked at... spied on, from at least two places. She thought. Her eyes fluttered open. From up here and from over there.

She looked again at the ledge in front of the caves. An almost transparent feather bedecked figure drifted in and out of the mouth of the cave. His dance steps seemed timed to the drum beats of the pounding rig.

Chapter 15

Seconds later the figure disappeared. Ellen continued to stare at the cave opening. She heard Merle's voice and tore her gaze from the hillside.

"Let's go on down, little lady," Merle began the climb down the crossbars.

Ellen crouched to start down. She found the first cross tie with her right foot, then the second with her left. She looked across the wooden platform of the monkey board before she released her hold on the low rail that banded the opening. When she put a foot onto the third cross member she froze in place, one hand still on the platform, the other on the first rung down. She had one foot on the third cross member and one foot in the air.

Her mind darted frantically, giving orders to her unmoving hands and feet.

"I can't make it," she muttered against the wood. She could feel the vibrating blow of the gray wood against her lips at each step Merle made downward. He can't hear me, she thought, and he's not looking up. He sure can't see me.

She closed her eyes to fight the impulse that filled her arms and legs. It was as if they were telling her, "Let go. Just fall. You can't make it." Her knuckles whitened against the weathered wood. "No," she whispered.

The warmth of a hand moved across Ellen's hair. She opened her eyes and looked up into the brown eyes of a young woman hovering in the air above her.

"Yahola," the name was a smothered breath from Ellen's lips. "Help me."

The Indian woman smiled

"You can climb down, Ellen." Yahola assured her. "I will stay with you as long as you need me. I will help you."

Ellen felt her chest thaw. She moved first one hand, then one leg onto the next rungs.

"Good," the face floated above her line of vision. "Now another, my cousin."

Ellen felt her way to another rung.

"Now, you can do it," the warm caress moved across her hair again and Ellen backed down the rest of the crossbars slowly but steadily. She felt the heavy thumps of the cable tool through the thin soles of her shoes when she pulled the ladder close enough to lower herself to the floor of the rig.

Merle stood a few feet away, talking to two of the men. He gestured to her and left the men standing as he leaped to the ground. He lifted his hands to indicate that she must jump into his arms from the rig floor. He moved his fingers to encourage her.

Ellen jumped and the oil man clutched her body to slide down his own.

She realized it was nothing like the feelings she had noted when Roman had lifted her down from his horse.

"Ready to go on in to Drumright?"

She nodded. Her gaze lifted to the monkey board high overhead. It was as if a long black skirt flashed in the wind and disappeared from the platform.

"She helped me," The words were only a faint whisper.

Merle pulled Ellen's hand through the crook of his elbow to walk to the Model T. "What'd you say, hon?'

"Yes. Let's go."

Merle cranked the car to life and both sat silently on the ride toward town until they passed Jake Linder's place. "Them Linders has gone Indian, some says," Merle muttered.

Ellen didn't answer and both remained silent until Merle maneuvered the car into a parking space on Broadway.

"Got to go upstairs to see Miss Grace Arnold. You want to come up with me, hon? "

I might as well go with him, she told herself. Ellen followed the oil man up the narrow stairway to the lawyer's office. Grace Arnold herself opened the door for them and motioned them to chairs. She walked into a second room then returned with a folder. She held it out to Ellen. "Here it is, Miss Wiley, our file on Half Hollow Hill."

Ellen turned, her astonishment clear in her voice. "Half Hollow Hill? I thought you had to see the lawyer about something?"

"Right, little lady. And what I had to see her about was your place. That's the main reason I wanted you to come in with me. Me and you has got to talk some business." He stood and walked to the window. "Remember? I told you that." He looked back at her and returned to his chair. "We're needing a lease on the land out in back of your house."

"The caves?"

"Yeah. All that hill back there . Might be a lot of oil, make yourself some money." He laughed. "You going to be rich, hon."

"But that's the Indian burial place. I'm supposed to watch after them..." Her voice trailed away.

"Now, I told you about all that Indian foolishness. Let's just..."

Grace Arnold cut in. "He's right, Miss Wiley. It would be very foolish to listen to a lot of claptrap about sacred burial grounds."

Ellen opened her mouth but no words came out.

"Besides," the oil man took up the argument, "If you think there is spirits up in there, they ain't nothing like a oil rig and a bunch of roughnecks to drive all them ghosts back to hell... or wherever they come from."

Ellen tried again. "The Indians don't want me to lease that land. It's very special to them."

"Your cousin Yahola wasn't so particular as all that." The woman lawyer's voice gained volume. "She didn't have anything against money."

"Nor oil men either," Merle grinned and tipped his chair back against the wall.

"Yahola signed a lease for you to drill for oil there?"

"Yep. Right where you was today, as a matter of fact. That's your land, too, you know." He tipped the chair forward and stood to pace again to the window, "Sacred spirits and all that is right there, too, I reckon. And we're drilling there. Ain't nothing stopped us yet once we sign a lease on a place."

"You shouldn't have to listen to all that nonsense the Indians spout," Grace Arnold's voice was quiet, business-like. "Of course, it is too bad she had to die there."

"Yahola? Died there? Where? At the oil rig?"

Merle's voice overrode her questions. "Grace, I guess we better get on back. My crew is short a man today so I'll have to be on the floor. I'll talk to the little lady and we'll get this all straightened out."

In the car, Ellen sat stiffly then questions burst from her lips.

"Merle, why did Yahola die there? At your rig? How? What happened?"

The oil man kept his eyes on the rutted track.

"Answer me. Why did she sign the lease to you? When did she die? How? Were you there?"

"Now, take it easy, little lady," He lifted one hand from the wheel and placed it over her hand that rested on the seat.

Ellen jerked her hand away. Her command was bitten out, word by word. "Tell. Me. What. Happened!"

"Well, okay. But I don't want to upset you."

"Upset me? I'm practically hysterical now. Just tell me everything, this very minute."

Merle pulled the car off to the side of the road.

"We was at the rig."

"Then you were with her when she died?"

"Yes. We was visiting the rig."

"What really happened?"

"I'm not exactly sure."

"But you were with her?"

"Well, yes. We was up on the catwalk. She fell..." Merle turned to look at Ellen, "Or maybe she jumped."

Ellen's fear of the climb down from the high monkey board returned full force. "She fell from the monkey board." Horror touched her words. "That's why she was up there with me!" Tears rose in her eyes.

"She didn't die right away," Merle continued, "We carried her into Drumright but there wasn't nothing they could do." He was silent for a moment. "She was kind of all broken up inside, they told us."

"Broken up," Ellen's words were a sob. "Oh my God." The last was a sigh.

Chapter 16

"Let me out at the schoolhouse, please, Merle." Ellen gestured toward the log structure just ahead.

"You going to work on a nice day like this, little lady?"

"Just a letter." Ellen felt the muscle in her left arm twitch slightly. All that climbing, she thought. "I have to hurry and work on a letter, a personal letter." She could hear her voice rising but she couldn't seem to control the sound. She needed to get away from this man and his constant "Little Lady," nonsense when he spoke to her.

"Okay, okay. You're going to write a letter. No need to lose your temper."

Ellen smiled at the oil man. "I didn't mean to sound angry. It's just that I suddenly feel as though I must hurry. My fingers are twitching to get to work."

"Well, here we are. Want me to come in with you?"

"No, no," she stepped down from the Model T, clanged the door shut and moved toward the school. "Thanks for my first car ride." She threw the words over her shoulder. When she reached the school she stood just inside the door until she no longer heard the engine of the Model T. In a second she was behind the teacher's desk where she pulled the green books from their resting place. She stacked them at the left corner of her desk.

"I'm going to finish this today." Her voice rang metallic with determination. "I'm not going to the house until I'm finished."

Words and paragraphs began to fill the first page when Ellen lifted her gaze. This is a diary, a story day by day! She bent again over the paper and books. She muttered as she searched and wrote.

"He... Yahola who is this 'he' you keep mentioning? Um... Guilty... Indian law... violated law." She raised her head. Her whisper filled the room. "There I go. Talking to myself again. What normal person does that?"

He, whoever he is, violated her somehow, and she thought she violated the laws of her people. She spoke about Yahola's words within her own mind.

Her work continued until Ellen couldn't see through her tears. Yahola wanted to die. Again she bent to the work. She lifted the edge of her yellow skirt to clear tears from her eyes. She's warning me, warning me that this "he" will try to play the same game with me. She pulled clean paper from the desk drawer. I've got to get all of this written neatly in chronological order, she thought, then maybe I can make some sense of it.

She didn't notice the silence deepening in the room nor the shadows lengthening. Her right hand flew over the new paper, stopping only to dip her pen into the inkwell. Her left hand searched the pages of the dark green books to hold her place at each lightly marked word.

"And I still don't know!" Ellen's words rang with anguish.

A tiny movement in front of her caused her to drop the pen and stare at the figure before her.

"Mr. Fixico... Roman," Her voice hung on a barb of shock. "Where did you come from? What do you want?"

The brown eyes stared at her but the Indian didn't speak. One dark hand moved to caress the desktop next to him.

"Well, what is it? How did you get in here?"

"I will ask you a question," His voice was so low it was almost soundless. "Why did you go to the caves without my permission?"

"Permission?" Anger rose in her, "First, Roman Fixico, I don't owe you an explanation for anything I do. You are not my keeper. And second, I certainly will not ask you nor anyone else for permission to do whatever I wish on my own property."

The last four words, on-my-own-property, were almost a whisper. She stared back at the unmoving Indian.

Seconds passed.

Roman moved toward the dais where she sat. Ellen felt pushed back into her chair by the fury that shone in the man's eyes. His voice was still soft but the words filled every corner of the room.

"Miss Wiley... Ellen Wiley, you may not understand this yet. Let me explain something to you. You, Ellen Wiley, owe me an explanation for everything you do... for everything you have done... for everything you plan to do."

Shock and rage struggled for possession of Ellen. Whatever has caused this man to think I need to have his permission for anything?

"You are crazy. Get out of here. Get out of my classroom." She moved from behind the desk, she pointed at the main entrance, "Get out! Get out! Get out!"

Roman turned toward the door. Before he opened it he turned back to look at her. "See what you have..."

Anger heated her blood. Rage shook her body.

"Get out of my classroom."

The Indian said a word Ellen did not understand and he closed the door behind himself without another sound.

Ellen raised her hand to her cheek. She could feel the heat behind her skin. She ran to stand in the place where Roman Fixico had stood, turned to look at the teacher's desk. She felt the wrath drain from her as if a faucet had been turned.

"What was wrong with me?" She asked aloud, "I don't understand. Why was I shouting at him?"

Chapter 17

Ellen stood in the aisle where Roman Fixico had been standing only moments before. She touched the desktops on either side of her as Roman had done. The wood felt strangely warm, as if it returned her touch.

"I'm acting so silly, imagining things again." she said aloud as she walked back up to the desk.

When she sank into the wooden teacher's chair, she stared for another moment at the spot where Roman had been then she looked once more at the books and papers before her. The turning of pages and the scratching of the pen against the paper were the only sounds for a time. Those soft writing sounds were drowned in Ellen's murmur of shock.

Almost all of it... I've got almost all of it. She looked again at the place where Roman had been standing. I just need a bit more information and then I'll know everything.

Her mind flashed a picture of the "R" volume of the green set of books. That lone book stood high on a shelf above the fireplace in the Fixico house.

"Oh, it's in his house," she murmured. She felt herself blushing. "Wouldn't you know?" So embarrassing. After running the man off that way, now I have to go to him, begging for that other book. She spoke aloud to give herself a bit of practice in abjectness. "Please, Mr. Fixico, if you'll let me have the book which you donated to the school I promise I won't run you off anymore." She had to laugh at her own sarcasm.

She sighed and looked at the paper before her. Well, I must go, she thought, there isn't any way I can finish this without the "R" volume.

She replaced the Books of Knowledge on the shelf, then tore all except one of the sheets of paper into several pieces.

She moved back to the pot bellied stove and opened it. The dark metal felt cold to the touch.

No one will be looking in here while it's still so warm, she thought, and when we light the first fire that will take care of that.

She returned to the desk and picked up the remaining sheet of paper. For a moment her eyes followed the words she had written then she folded the tablet paper and looked about the room. She stopped again at the desk. She pulled out each drawer and looked inside. She shook her head and continued to hold the paper in her hand.

"What shall I do with this?"

She touched her chin with the folded sheet, shrugged and folded the square into an even smaller rectangle then lifted her hem and pulled her rolled stocking top loose. With a quick movement of both hands she folded the paper several more times then fixed the small wad within the silk. She twisted the hose top sharply and turned the small lump under.

"There," She smiled at the neat hiding place in the stocking and patted the lump. "Easy to carry, hard to find."

I'll go through the hill path to the Fixico's, she decided. I can be there in a few minutes, get the book and finish Yahola's message before total dark. Her steps slowed as she reviewed the moments earlier when she had screamed at the Indian to leave. Again she felt embarrassment rising.

I'll just be very civil, she decided, I'll demand the "R" volume then thank him and come straight back here. At her house she stepped into the kitchen to lift a drink from the wooden bucket which rested on the cabinet back of the pump. She replaced the dipper in the bucket and called.

"Uconthla?"

No answer.

"Conzey?"

The house around her stood silent. Better if they don't know where I'm going, she thought. She stepped out the back door and looked up toward the caves. She stared then raised her hand to shade her eyes. That's where they were.

"Uconthla?" Her words were a whispered question, "Conzey?" for a moment she watched the two old people above her. She could hear their chant. Conzey's hand lifted to make a sign in the air. Uconthla turned her back to his symbol and made the same sign toward the mouth of the cave.

"What...?" the word drifted from Ellen's mouth. She watched and listened for a moment, then shouted the word at the two on the ledge.

"What? Conzey? Uconthla? What's going on?"

The old people ignored her. Their chanting rose to a higher pitch and the symbols seemed to be written in the air with redoubled speed.

Ellen's mouth set into a thin line of determination. She strode across the yard and out to the path that led to the caves directly above.

"I'm coming up there!"

I'm going, she thought, and I'm going to force some sense out of those two people if it is the last thing I do. I have plenty to ask them and they are going to answer.

About Yahola... and about those caves... not to mention Mr. Fixico, the local big shot... and no more chanting nonsense. The words seemed to resound in her mind in short bursts. They are going to tell me everything I want to know and right now!

She rushed onto the path. The chanters fell silent but she could still see the two old Indians making frantic signs at the edge of the ledge.

"And none of that Creek stuff," she muttered and fixed her gaze on the Indians as if they were listening to her, "Plain English and plenty of it!"

Blackjack saplings slapped the air in the path as Ellen continued her climb. She could hear the voices of the old people again but she didn't slow down.

"I'll give them something to chant about," she said and looked up toward the ledge. The two were hidden from her view but she could hear them clearly.

English, she thought, that's English. They're speaking English.

"Miss Ellen. You no come. Go back."

"Not time yet. No come."

Ellen stopped a moment to listen and catch her breath.

"Better go back home, Miss Ellen."

"Go back. Go back."

Ellen half turned to look back at the house but she pushed a small branch that hung at eye level and resumed her climb.

"Not this time," she said, "Here I come with both eyes open."

The quality of the shouts changed to the strange language.

They think speaking Creek will keep me away, she told herself and she pulled herself around the last boulder in the path. When she could stand upright she looked toward the ledge where she was almost face to face with the two old people.

Their hands were now making signs that plainly said, "Go back. Go back."

"Not on your tintype," Ellen muttered and pulled herself up onto the ledge. She moved to within a few feet of the couple. Each of them still seemed to be warding her away from the cave entrance.

"Stop this foolishness, at once," Ellen's voice sounded weak in her own ears. "Tell me right now what you are doing and what is going on."

"We help the spirits of our ancestors," Uconthla moved and whispered to Ellen, "Ancestors live in cave. We guard their place."

Ellen took a step forward and both Indians stepped directly into her path. "We are chosen."

"What does that mean, 'You are chosen?'"

"Our people, our tribe. They choose us for sacred place. We keep white eyes away. Keep them from doing bad thing in sacred place."

"You mean white people desecrate the burial place of your ancestors?"

"White eyes bad for old ones. Roman say. Keep all away."

"Even the owner of the hill?" Ellen's turned her gaze toward the cave entrance.

"He say you not ready. Cave not ready. Old ones not ready. Plenty trouble."

The old man shoved himself into Ellen's line of vision.

"I will tell," He pushed Uconthla toward the drums, "You drum."

Ellen felt real surprise. He can speak English, she thought, so why is he always silent?

Conzey's eyes closed a moment then opened to look heavenward. He lifted both hands to shoulder level then spread them in an expansive outward movement.

Ellen watched, fascinated by the fluid movements. He doesn't even look old now, she thought.

Conzey spoke in a singsong monotone.

"We walk through grass and tree. We drink sweet water. We speak to all as brothers. We honor old ones. Life is a moment on the true journey to the sky. We are happy."

The old man's arms dropped to his sides. The movement was slow as if he demonstrated defeat.

"Then, white eyes. White eyes come."

Ellen felt rooted to the spot. Her eyes glazed as if her stare would never break away from the man's moving mouth. She heard words but she did not understand. The sound rose, became a shout.

"What is it?" then answered silently, "He's speaking Creek."

She heard her own name in the rumble of strange words that fell from Conzey's lips.

Ellen stared but could not move.

Again Conzey raised his hands, this time in a twisting, tearing movement. The air in front of him seemed to wrestle the man's grasp. Again he used English.

"Betrayal!" His word was loud. "Old ones betrayed."

Ellen felt her mind close to real understanding. She became a stone, a stone with eyes, a stone with a brain. She heard the pain in Conzey's voice but she did not comprehend that pain. She struggled to awaken from the trance. "What is happening to me?" Her words were a murmur lost in the drumming and the throb of the old man's speech.

His tirade continued. Now English, now Creek. Ellen felt herself drowning in the flood of words. Once again she heard the shouted word, "Betrayed!"

"Not me," she wanted to shout, "I'm not the one who betrayed you."

Conzey and Uconthla began to speak in unison as they turned toward the cave entrance. Their arms rose and fell in a slow rhythm. Conzey lifted a feather from his hair and touched it to the drum, then to Ellen's mouth.

Ellen shrieked with fear but no sound came from her frozen stone lips.

"God help me," she prayed inwardly, "Something bad is happening to me. I can't move."

The feather descended again to the drum then pointed toward the place where she had recently stood with Roman.

Uconthla drummed with one hand as she touched Ellen with the other.

"Roman. You understand, girl. Roman. We speak his real name, but it is Roman." Again the feather pointed toward the Fixico farm.

The voices of the two old people rose to shouts and the drumming was a frenzy of sound.

Ellen tried to push herself backward to the edge of the ledge. Still stone, she could not move. She tried to turn her eyes from the two shouting Indians, but she could not.

Suddenly, the drumming stopped. Conzey dropped to one knee and placed the feather with the tip pointed toward the cave opening. At the same moment Uconthla placed her forehead against the drum and crouched in a stooping position.

The silence pushed against Ellen's ears.

Pale wisps of fire whirled from the cave and with it the dancer Ellen had seen before. His body gleamed in the firelight. Ellen could see the rock of the cave entrance through his body, Even so, he was real. He danced and weaved before the two old people who did not look at him. The dancer's eyes raked Ellen with a hard glitter. Inside her mind she could hear the beat of many drums and songs from many throats. Amazed that she was released from being stone she swayed with the sound.

The tall naked man stepped through the two old Indians and whirled to land on the ledge just in front of Ellen. Paint on his chest pulsated with his breath. The muscles under the painted skin writhed with his movements.

Ellen felt her own arms lift toward the dancer. He beckoned. She followed. Again he whirled and called to her. She stumbled forward. Her foot touched the crouching Uconthla, but Ellen hardly noticed. Her eyes were fixed upon the warrior. The man danced into the entryway of the cave.

"Wait," the words were torn from her, "Wait for me."

Her words lifted Uconthla to her feet.

"No, Miss Ellen," she touched Ellen's shoulder, "Not go."

Ellen shrugged off her the old woman's touch without looking at her.

"Don't leave me," she called to the tall Indian who swayed just inside the entryway.

"Conzey," Uconthla's grunted word pulled the old man to Ellen's other side.

"No go," he whispered, "Watch, but no go."

Ellen tugged herself forward to enter the cave but the two sets of hands held her firmly. "No go!"

Ellen watched the whirling Indian make a last leap and disappear into the darkness of the cave. His loss was almost physical pain for her. He'd been the most beautiful man she'd ever seen. His nudity had been enchanting rather than shocking. Now she knew how a man looked without clothing, how Roman would look without clothing.

"He's gone," she whispered. Tears rose in her eyes.

"Yes. Long ago," Uconthla spoke into her ear, "You only see an old one's spirit."

"He was beautiful."

Uconthla and Conzey massaged Ellen's arms. She felt the blood begin to course through her veins. She turned to the old woman in a dazed effort at understanding.

"He wanted me to go with him."

"Roman say, no go."

As the three stood staring into the cave a distant boom rose from the bowels of the hillside.

"That was in the cave," Ellen shouted. She pulled her arms from the grasp of the old people and ran toward the sound. As she ran another boom sounded more faintly this time.

"Someone is in there," she muttered and she stepped into the darkness of the cave.

Uconthla and Conzey did not move but stood staring after her.

Chapter 18

Ellen stopped to let her eyes adjust to the dim interior of the cave. She turned to look back. The two old people had not moved. They stood looking into the cave entrance. Neither made a sound when another boom echoed up from the bowels of the cave but they turned toward each other then walked away. Ellen watched until they were out of sight then she started inching forward again.

"No need to panic," she told herself, "I can still see pretty well."

The back of the cave narrowed to a passageway. Ellen reached to touch the wall on her right. The dry sandstone felt substantial. Her fingers were reassured by the harsh reality of the sandy roughness.

"This is my cave, after all," she murmured, "I'm not trespassing." She moved slowly but steadily into the passageway that slanted downward into the hillside. "Nothing to be afraid of." She ignored the weakness in her legs, the lifting of the hair on the back of her neck.

"My own cave," she said aloud. Her voice felt muffled in the close vestibule of stone. She looked back. The brightness of the sun filled entryway left an afterimage on her retina when she turned back to the tunnel. Again her hand reached to the stone wall for reassurance while she waited for her eyes to adjust once more to the gloom. Two steps and she stopped, then three more steps took her sharply down. She looked back. Only the topmost part of the entry way was visible now.

Mama used to say I had eyes like a cat, she reassured herself and she moved further down the incline. Abruptly, the dimness became solid darkness. She could distinguish the tunnel ahead only because it was a deeper black.

I'll let the cave wall guide me, she thought and reached again to touch the uneven sandstone. Her hand brushed against a sharply defined edge then into a space that seemed gouged into the solid wall. At the side of the indentation, Ellen felt a piece of wood.

Wood? her senses queried then answered, as she put up both hands to explore the find. A torch, maybe. A rag is tied to the wood. For the first time she became aware of the strong odor that rose from what she'd found to be a bundle of torches. Oil. They've soaked this cloth in some kind of oil so the torches will burn.

Torches, but no matches... shall I go back for something to light one of these? Her hands busily assessed the find, then she reached behind the neatly stacked wooden sticks. What? Her fingers moved forward again. Something else?

She felt compelled to run, run back to the sunlight, back to the open Oklahoma sky, but she stood her ground.

She closed her eyes and touched again. Fur? Hair? She screamed and backed away then leaned against the wall to catch her breath. Had that been hair? She forced herself to take a deep breath and to begin again her probe of the niche in the wall.

It didn't feel alive, she told herself. It won't bite you. There was something strange there. Was that a braid?

Her hand dared into the hole and grabbed a handful of the hair. She snatched it from the niche and ran toward the entryway. At the top of the incline she stopped and examined her find in the pale light. She lifted the bundle of hair toward the light. Part of it fell to the floor. She was left holding a braid. A long black braid. Two longer braids lay across her shoes.

She frowned. Strange. Braided hair... braided black hair... Indian hair? Thoughts jumbled through her mind. Who left braided hair here? The old ones?

Shock coursed through her. Braided Indian hair. Or at least hair braided to look like an Indian's hair. "A wig!" she said aloud. She stooped to pick up the braid that lay across her feet. There were two there, one with a feather attached in the braid. The hair was really smooth, shining, human hair, attached to a caplike piece of black cloth.

Ellen felt anger rising. That Roman, she thought, or those others. Everything I saw before was some kind of weird joke, I suppose. Memory of the firelit warrior dancing in and out of the mouth of the cave swept over her. "Crazy Indians," her words were almost a cry of pain, "They're trying to scare me."

One after another, pictures of the people she had seen dancing in the firelight swept into her mind.

How did they do that? she asked herself, How did they make themselves look transparent? She gave the three wig braids a shake.

Well, we'll just see what old Uconthla and Conzey have to say about this. All that nonsense about the "old ones," all that chanting... nothing but a hoax. A joke on the city-girl-schoolmarm."

She felt exhausted, drained. The walk to the outside ledge seemed never-ending. Everything in the cave looked flat, one dimensional, as though all the walls were painted scenery for a play.

They didn't need to go to all this trouble, she thought, and sighed. I'll leave. I'll go see Miss Grace Arnold in the morning. She can sell this place ... or give it to them if she wants to do that.

She looked down at the hair she carried. I couldn't stay here. Not now. Now that I know.

Light flooded into the large room. Ellen tried to move faster, to get out of the cave. Her feet refused to obey. She felt as though she were trying to push herself through a thick transparent liquid, pushing and getting nowhere. The open entry lay just yards in front of her but she felt as if she could never make it out. The flat, "painted-looking" walls suddenly sharpened into roughly hewn rock. The sandy floor unfolded into crevices and bowl-like depressions. A fire glowed in the center of the entryway.

"Uconthla, Conzey," the names formed in her mind but her throat made no sound. She licked her lips and tried again. "Help," but she heard nothing, nothing except the drumming. She turned toward the drums at the inner wall of the cave. Several men sat pounding the drums they held in the center of their circle. Ellen inched toward the wall on her right.

"Oh no," Her voice was again drowned in the sound. Tall figures leaped from the dark passageway to circle the fire. The naked warrior she had seen before moved to the center of the dancing ring of men and his leaps and turns drove the others to greater frenzy. Now, voices, a singing chant, filled the cavern.

Ellen pressed herself as closely to the rock as possible. She dropped the wigs and stood transfixed as once again the huge golden man danced and beckoned to her. The sunlit entry was dark now and the firelight bounced a reflection of the flames from the quartz chips that glinted within the rock walls. Tall shadows thrust themselves across the rocks and enveloped Ellen in their warmth.

At a word she did not know but which she understood, Ellen straightened and moved toward the fire, toward the tall warrior. He stood with his back to the fire, a black silhouette outlined with flame, a shadow of immense power. He stood and waited for her coming. Ellen made one step toward the waiting figure, then stopped for a moment. He raised one arm, and again beckoned. She moved forward another step.

"Ellen."

Ellen ignored the unwanted interruption. She took another step toward the figure before the fire.

"Ellen, come on out."

She took another step. She raised her hands, one to each side of her head to cover her ears.

I wish whoever that is would go away, Ellen thought, this is too important. I don't want to miss any of this. She moved another step closer to the figure outlined with flame.

"Ellen. Come on out of there, little lady."

The figures of the circling Indians seemed to soften at the edges.

"Ellen. It's getting late. You come on up here now. We're waiting on you."

The figure of the beckoning man faded.

Ellen hurried her next step.

"Miss Schoolmarm. Come on."

The dancers, the drums, the black figure, the fire turned to mist and vanished. Ellen ran three steps, then stopped. She searched the huge room and tears came to her eyes.

"They've gone," her voice was a cry of despair. "They've left me behind."

Merle's voice was clear now. "Ellen. Come on or I'm going to come in and get you."

Ellen sighed. It was his voice that did it, she thought, Merle's voice drove them away. She turned toward the entry way.

Chapter 19

Ellen opened her eyes and stared at the bedroom ceiling. In a moment all the happenings of the day before pushed a jumble of questions into her mind. The moments high up in the rig, learning about Yahola's death, the message from the books, the cave... Ellen clamped down on the intruding thoughts.

I'm not going to worry about it, I would like to talk all that over with Roman. I may be falling in love with the man. I think that's what made me so angry. He has done nothing but good things for me. She continued to lie unmoving in the bed, her gaze fastened upon a heavy ceiling beam. Mama was wrong to try to make me fear Indians. Roman. She wished she could see him. Right now. The man in the cave had looked so much like him! She felt her cheeks flush at the memory of the beautiful naked man who had looked so much like Roman and again imagined how Roman would look with no clothing. A long moment later she pushed the sheet back and stood.

Today, she promised herself, Today, I'll get something settled, something done. I'll go back to the cave first of all.

Voices and movement from the kitchen hurried her into choosing a green plaid cotton dress that sported a black patent leather belt at the hipline. Too short, Uconthla would say. Her mother had also said, "Too short." But mama had liked the color with her red hair. She pulled a brush through her curls and hardly glanced at the mirror. She tiptoed to the door and lifted the latch without a sound. She held the knob in one hand, the latch in the other and pushed a crack to peek through.

Merle stood with his back toward her. His voice came clearly from the kitchen doorway. The voices of the old couple were only muffled sounds.

"Well, I got the lawyer here."

Conzey spoke but Ellen could not make out his words.

"I'm going to see Ellen anyhow. Lawyer Grace Arnold came all the way out here and Miss Ellen's going to meet with us. It don't matter what you think."

Again there was a flurry of sound from the old Indians.

Merle turned to move down the dogtrot toward Ellen's bedroom and a hand reached from the kitchen doorway and grasped his arm to pull him back inside the room.

What's going on? Ellen mouthed the words to herself.

She closed the door and leaned against it. All the earlier questions rose, demanding answers. And now there was some kind of fuss here. She scooped her pocketbook from the dresser and opened the bedroom wide.

"Merle," she called as she walked, "You're early."

The voices in the kitchen quieted and the oil man appeared at the kitchen door. He smiled at Ellen and rested his weight against the door frame leaning against his right hand.

"I come to get you to go to the rig again today, little lady. Got us some business to talk about."

There was no sound from Uconthla and Conzey.

Ellen ducked under the oil man's uplifted arm and into the kitchen. Uconthla stood at her usual place at the stove. Conzey wasn't in the room.

"No breakfast, Uconthla. I think I'll go with Mr. Caudill, then later I'm going up to the caves."

Uconthla didn't turn to look at Ellen. Ellen shrugged and turned to Merle. The oil man's smile seemed to jump back into place.

"Let's go then, little lady."

Ellen walked just out of range of the oil man's touch as they crossed the small yard to the waiting Model T. Ellen looked up at the cave ledge above while Merle worked to start the car.

Just a sunny ledge, she thought, nothing unusual at all.

When they arrived at the rig she saw a blue buggy powered by a sorrel pony parked near the blackjacks at the edge of the rig clearing. When the Model T came close a woman stepped down from the buggy.

"Grace Arnold," Merle explained as if Ellen were not able to recognize her. The lawyer stood beside her buggy and waited for them to come to her. Ellen could see a bundle of papers in the woman's hand.

"I sent one of the boys into town yesterday to get her out here. He told her we was wanting to talk a little business with her today."

"The oil lease," Ellen's words came out unbidden.

"Yeah, that's it." Merle's tone was admiring. "You're a sharp little lady."

Ellen opened the car door before the oil man could reach her side of the car.

"Good morning, Miss Arnold. Welcome to Half Hollow Hill."

The older woman tilted her face toward the sun before she spoke. "I use every excuse I can to get out of that office, Miss Wiley. I especially love Yahola's... your place... out here. It's so peaceful." The lawyer smiled at Ellen. "And I love the Oklahoma sun. Have you learned to love it, too?"

Ellen nodded. "You'd think nothing bad could ever happen in a place where the sun floods down like this," her voice was a lazy murmur. "My mother tried to keep me out of the sun her whole life. Said it would ruin my white skin."

"Has something bad happened?" the lawyer's voice was a murmur, also.

"Nothing bad happened," the oil man's voice cut in, "Schoolmarm had a busy day yesterday, is all."

Both women continued to face the sun, eyes closed.

"Uhmm-m-m." Ellen's sigh caused both to smile and open their eyes to look at the oil man. "What can I do for you, Miss Arnold?"

"Mr. Caudill asked me to come out with these papers."

"Why don't we go sit by the doghouse?" the oil man asked, "Might as well be comfortable."

Ellen walked, head down, picking her way through the tufts of coarse grass. Dust sifted over the toes of her white slippers. She's right, Ellen agreed, there is a lot to love down here in Oklahoma. Maybe someday... Roman's face slid through her mind... maybe someday... she didn't finish her thought.

"Sit down, ladies." Merle put opened newspapers on the bench built along the outside of the little tin house which had been built for the drilling crew.

Ellen sat and motioned the lawyer to sit beside her. Merle stood in front of them.

'The little lady already knows what we was going to talk about." he said.

"Well, not really." Ellen's voice held a question.

"I had Grace get the papers ready for you."

"What papers?"

"You know. I talked about it. I need your signature before we can drill up on the hill."

"At the caves you mean?"

"Yeah, we talked about it."

"Well, Merle, I really haven't had time to think about it." Ellen reached for the sheaf of papers the other woman held. "Let me see what you want me to do. I told Roman we would keep the drilling away from the Hill, Merle. I can't just sign..."

"Nothing to think about," the oil man interrupted. "You sign, we drill. You get a big chunk of money when we strike. Never mind what you said to Fixico. Just do what I say little lady."

Chapter 20

Ellen looked at the papers, then at the lawyer. She won't be any help, Ellen thought, to her it's just business... nothing special, only one more land deal near Drumright.

"I'll give your proposal some thought," Ellen clutched the papers against her chest, "And I'll let you know."

"Let's all go up on the rig and I'll show you just the places I got in mind for the drilling." Merle Caudill's voice was velvety.

Ellen stood to look up at the platform overhead. She shivered and shook her head. "No thanks."

"Come on little lady. I can make everything real clear up there." He turned toward the lawyer. "How about you, Grace? Want to see Half Hollow Hill from up high?"

The lawyer stood and pulled on white gloves. "Not now, Merle. I must be going." She didn't look toward Ellen when she spoke. "Miss Wiley, I'm sorry, I just can't bear high places." She moved quickly to the blue buggy.

Ellen felt as though Miss Arnold was apologizing for something that had nothing to do with height. The lawyer waved once after her horse had trotted toward the main road, then she and her buggy disappeared in the dust thrown from under the wheels of her vehicle.

Ellen and Merle stood watching the lawyer's departure. Neither spoke until the oil man broke the silence.

"Well, come on little lady. Up you go."

Ellen shook her head. "Not me. I am not going up there again!"

"Hm. I feel sorry for you, kiddo. Now you're acting like one of them old fashioned goody-two-shoe ladies. Here I thought you was so proud of being an independent career woman of the twenties!"

***

Ellen stared down at her dust covered slippers. She watched her right foot step forward, then her left. Her gaze locked onto the movement as if she were watching two strange objects, animate objects not seen before. Her feet's movement continued to the ladder and across to the wooden crossbars.

"Atta girl!" The oilman's voice shattered against the wind. "Right on up to the top with you!"

Shouts and calls from below filtered only vaguely up to Ellen's consciousness. Her arms and legs continued to move mechanically up and up.

"Dill, Dill!" The calls from below became more urgent but Ellen did not falter in the climb.

Her movement from ladder to cross tie, then on up to the next cross tie seemed to have become the beall and endall of Ellen's existence.

Finally, at eye level with the floor of the monkey board platform Ellen stared across the square platform. The sunlight on the rough wood seemed heavy, heated, thick, almost green, as if she had gone underwater rather than up into the air.

Somehow Ellen felt no surprise to see the Indian woman standing on the monkey board floor. The woman's dark hair and her dark skirt appeared to float in the liquid light. Yahola smiled and motioned toward Ellen, encouraging her to continue the climb.

"Yahola," Ellen breathed the name and hurried up the last three rungs, "Yahola, you're here."

Her cousin nodded and smiled even more widely. The beautiful Indian woman's voice seemed to shimmer in the lighted haze of the platform. Ellen's thought moved to Roman's face. Are all Indians beautiful? She wondered.

"My cousin. My young cousin. You are here."

Ellen scrambled up the last step and pulled herself to stand on the platform.

"Yahola, I've been trying to write out your message."

The floating figure again smiled and nodded. "I know. My warning. I was thrown from here." She glided to a point on the side facing the cave ledges. "From this very place." Ellen could see the guy wire that stretched down into the woods.

Ellen's hand covered her mouth then slid to her cheek. Her voice whispered horror. "Thrown from up here?"

"Thrown or jumped, they say. It does not matter now. I betrayed our people." Yahola quickened her pace about the perimeter of the platform. "You," the woman's face distorted with urgency, "You, Ellen Wiley..."

Ellen moved back a step, trying to escape Yahola's vehemence, her pointing finger.

"What is it?" Ellen's voice quivered in her throat.

"Now you are the guardian. I can do nothing more. The old ones..." Yahola gestured toward the cave. "The old ones sent me. This is the meeting place. Right here. On the ground where this thing stands. They want their place."

Ellen looked at the ledge above the house. The flames of a fire reflected against the tanned bodies of the naked dancers. One of them stood with arms upraised against the sky. He faced toward the rig and Ellen felt as though his gaze reached across the distance to touch her face.

"He's watching me," she whispered.

As she spoke the boards beneath her feet seemed to tip slightly then settle back into place, the hand-hold on the cable jangled with the movement. The movement was followed by the tiny rocking motion of the whole structure. Through the thin soles of her graduation slippers, strong vibrations danced up into Ellen's legs. The rig moved once again, this time swaying strongly. A rumbling sound came from someplace below the spot where she stood.

Below, in the open space near the doghouse, Ellen could see that Jake's wagon had moved into the area near the rig. She gasped when Roman slid from the wagon seat before Jake had fully stopped the vehicle. Maybe he was here to rescue her?

Ellen stared down at the two men. They looked like dolls, dolls who were moving. Their mouths opened and closed, their hands waved toward her but she could hear nothing. Caught up in the whirling strangeness of the monkey board, Ellen shifted closer to the edge of the small platform.

As she watched the tiny actors below, an automobile raced into the clearing. She could see the word painted on the side of the large touring car: "Sheriff." Two men wearing badges stepped from the car and joined Roman and Jake to stare up at her. The sheriff brought the Chief of Police, Ellen thought. She'd heard of Jack Ary, could it be Ary with the sheriff?

At the ladder opening Merle's head appeared. He scrambled up onto the monkey board platform and grabbed Ellen around the waist. He shouted instructions to her but Ellen couldn't understand his words. He pulled her toward the cable that ran rigidly at an angle to the ground to disappear out in the woods somewhere.

Ellen tried to fight off the oilman's hands but he dragged her closer to the platform edge where the handhold was secured. He wrapped his left arm around Ellen and lifted her against him, then scissored her body within his legs. With his right hand he gripped the handhold and leaned out into the air with Ellen secured against his body.

He shouted and Ellen thought she heard the word, "Oil!"

They hung in the air for a second then Merle jerked the handhold into movement. Ellen could not reach high but she clasped her lower arms around the man's waist. They began their descent, faster and faster, both suspended from the oilman's right arm that gripped the handhold. The trees and the ground sped toward them and Ellen closed her eyes to keep from seeing death as it rose toward her.

The metal handhold shrieked against the steel cable for two hundred feet down into the woods. She felt pain from the brush and dried plants tearing at her legs and arms. She heard her skirt rip and felt her shoes drag in the sand filled pit just before the oil man dropped the handhold, and released Ellen. He tumbled and rolled into a large purple thistle bush. Ellen lay silent in the sand pit, breath knocked from her.

As she lay staring up into the leafy branches of a blackjack tree, the ground shifted and the sound of a hundred cannons split the air.

So, this is what it's like to be dead? She thought.

Chapter 21

A drop of heavy liquid splashed on Ellen's cheek. She lifted her hand to touch it and opened her eyes to see the sky darkened with a flaring spread of the black substance. She looked more carefully at her finger. Before she could say anything, Merle reached to touch the drop on her face and his murmured word, "Oil," explained the noise and the rain of dark droplets.

In the next instant he had grabbed her arm and lifted her to her feet. "Come on here, kiddo, you're going to be my ticket out of here." He half carried, half dragged her further into the woods, away from the rig.

She let herself go limp. Maybe he would go on and leave her alone is he thought he'd have to carry her.

He shook her roughly. "Wake up, little lady. You're going to have to walk." In moments he had pushed her to go ahead of him on the narrow path which he pointed out.

"Merle, why are you doing this?"

Ellen felt sickness rising from her stomach, cold sweat beaded on her forehead. She let her knees give way and she watched the underbrush rise up to meet her face as if the fall were happening to someone else. The oilman jerked her upright again and Ellen bent to vomit into the pathway. When she'd finished she wiped her mouth with the back of her hand and turned to look at her abductor.

"Why are you doing this?"

Her only answer was a shove to continue in the direction they had started. The hike was an agony of torn skin, harsh shoves from the oil man and a constant desire to again spit out the bile which rose in her mouth.

The path rose steadily before them and in minutes, Ellen had to use outcroppings and root growths to help pull herself upward.

"We're going to the caves!" The words escaped her before she could stop them.

"Right!" came the grunt from behind her and a finger jabbed into her ribs sped her onward in her climb.

"The sheriff was there to get *you*."

"Well, he ain't getting me. Not unless he wants you dead, little lady. I ain't worried."

Ellen peered back at the oil man and his slitted eyes glittered blue ice up at her. "We got us a place. Up there." He pointed over Ellen's shoulder and again shoved her forward.

As if a light turned on in Ellen's head she again saw the braided wigs and the bundled torches at the cave. Another picture swam across her consciousness. The Indians... burning the school... riding away.

"I found your wigs." Her words were meant to stop him but they did not.

"I know that, girl. Get on up there."

The climb steepened sharply. Pushed from the back, Ellen pulled herself up, ignoring the cuts on her hands, the bruises on her shins. An almost vertical wall lay before her and Ellen slumped against the wall, facing her tormentor.

"Why have you been courting me if you only want to harm me?"

Caudill leaned against the wall beside her and caught his own breath.

"Well, little lady... It was either marry you or scare you off. I tried both." He lifted a lock of her hair and Ellen moved away from his touch. "But you was a stubborn little gal. I had to get you off dead center... get you moving somehow." He sighed and yawned. "I had to take stronger measures. Anyway, it's not you I want, it's your land... and what's under it." Again he lifted the lock of red hair. "But that's not to say I would say 'no' if you was to offer. But what the hell, now I got you and the oil and all I have to do is get you to call off the dogs, right?"

Ellen tried to inch away from the man's touch but the space would allow little movement.

"Ain't nobody going to disturb us up yonder." He pointed and moved behind Ellen to boost her upward. "Let's get going now."

Ellen scrambled up the incline and felt her dress catch to rip again as she climbed. Uconthla's going to be upset, she thought and she wished she could hear the old woman berating her just one more time for tearing her "too short" dress.

On the narrow ledge she stood up and Caudill pulled himself up to stand beside her. "Now we're going to move to the right, then up again." Caudill pointed to the narrow foothold and Ellen followed his instructions.

If I can get to the ledge above the house, she told herself, someone will see me. She started upward again at the man's silent gesture.

Within minutes they emerged from the rocks and brush to stand in the mouth of a cave. The floor of the cave and the cave opening were hidden by the growth of trees and bushes around it.

"This isn't where we came the other day?"

Caudill snickered.

"You might say it's the back door, little lady."

The floor of the cave sloped upward and Ellen realized that the cave somehow intersected with the caverns which opened onto the ledge above her house.

As darkness closed in upon them Caudill stopped her with a command and Ellen could hear his hands searching on the stone surface as she had searched on the day she'd found the wigs.

"Got it!" He struck a match and held it to the torch he carried in his other hand. He handed the burning torch to Ellen and lifted another to touch the flame she held.

"Now you can see the little hideout me and the boys fixed up."

Ellen prayed for enough courage to run, to try to hide away without the torch to betray her but she knew she could not face the thick darkness alone, would have to stay with this vile man in the frightening half light of the flickering torches.

At each branch of the tunnel Caudill indicated the right hand passage until at last they turned to the left at one of the openings and stepped into a huge circular room. Caudill stepped to a torch fixed to the wall and lit it from the one he held in his hand. He gestured with a flourish.

"All the comforts of home."

Several mattress ticks lay piled to one side, a central circle of rocks had obviously been used for cooking. Pans and dishes wee stacked nearby. A small stream trickled through one side of the room and out another. A huge mass of wood lay cut and stockpiled across from the stream. A mirror winked and glittered under the flaring torch set into the wall. Below the looking glass a table with pots and jars stood as if on a ladies dressing table. The oil man smirked and opened a jar to dip a finger into it and stroke a red Z across his cheek.

"Me Indian," he shouted and laughed.

"Maybe they'll hear us," Ellen wished she had the guts to run and ram her torch into the man's face. "I just can't" she told herself. "Surely they'll hear him."

As if he could read her mind, the oil man boomed out a war cry, then laughed again.

"Can't nobody hear us," he said and smiled at her, "Nor find us either... not until I'm good and ready for them to find us. It's just you and me, baby. How about that?" The oil man's smile was a leer now and Ellen felt herself shrinking inwardly. Questions tumbled through her mind.

What does he intend to do with me? How can I defend myself? Can I escape somehow? Can I make myself attack him?

Caudill moved toward her. To Ellen it was as if he slithered across the stone floor. He took the burning branch from her hand and set in a holder high to her right. He put his own torch into a third holder.

"Now," He seemed pleased, "Now we can get better acquainted."

Ellen shuddered. Cold in here, she thought, and I'm afraid. That's why my knees feel as if they're going to give way. She pressed herself against the rock wall and let herself slip to a sitting position with the wall supporting her.

"Could we have a fire?"

"You betcha little lady. Nobody works good when they're cold." He jumped the tiny stream, lifted a double armload of wood and crossed back with another leap almost as agile as the first. He whistled as he clattered the log chunks to the floor then busied himself starting a fire inside the circle of stones.

He's awfully strong, Ellen thought, and he's at home here. The only way I'll ever get away from him it to outsmart him. Or... maybe Roman will...? But she squelched that thought.

Better not depend on anyone else, she knew she'd have to save herself if she could.

As her captor bustled about, at ease in the area, Ellen felt herself sinking into unthinking apathy. Nothing to be done... nothing. Her mind drifted. Caudill's voice called her back to the hard rock floor where she sat. What was he talking about? Yahola? He chattered away as if he were entertaining a guest at home.

"...and I don't mind telling you even if she was an Indian, that little old Yahola was a real woman. Too much like most women for my taste. Kept after me about marriage after we done that thing, you see?" He looked over his shoulder at Ellen. "I didn't go into it for anything like that. Sleeping with her was fine, but the lease was what I was after." He shook his head regretfully. "Too bad I had to see she was taken care of... didn't know she was going to go and get someone to take her place. You, of course. We just wanted her gone." His glance at Ellen held speculation. "Did you really think we was a gang of Indians that set fire to the schoolhouse?"

"Yes. I really thought so." Ellen's voice sounded rusty and unused. "I didn't guess any of your secrets. I suppose I'm just stupid."

The oil man looked pleased at her response. "Naw. Just a little city girl. More like innocent. Pretty little thing, too... wish I didn't have to..." his voice trailed into nothingness.

He means he is going to have to kill me, she warned herself, I have to do *something*. Lassitude crept over her again. The male voice, the murmur of the stream, the popping of the burning wood seemed to recede into the distance. Moments later, Ellen realized she could see the whole cave room as if she were perched somewhere near the ceiling. She could even see her own body slumped against the wall, eyes half closed, breathing slowed almost to nothing. What's happening? I can see everything, hear everything but I'm up here looking down at myself?

She made a tentative movement to see what Merle Caudill carried toward the fire. A pan. Filled with batter. He's fixing supper! Ellen felt incredulous excitement fill her. I can see everywhere... without moving... I'm out of my body!

In the moment of the thought Ellen looked out at the log house from the ledge at the side of the cave which faced her house and the school. How did I get here? Ellen veered back to the round stone room where her body sat still slumped against the wall. The oil man still moved about preparing food.

I can go anywhere, she thought but she felt drawn to the body waiting below. What if I left it there? Would I be dead? What is happening?

A shimmering figure joined her in her survey of the scene in the round cavern. Then another. Ellen did not speak but their thoughts intermingled with hers.

More of the Indian figures surrounded her and it was as if they advised her.

"You are one of us."

"You must go back. We need you to stay with our place."

"Roman is searching for you now."

"We will give you special powers it you will return."

"It is written that you will have a long life with Roman."

As if a cork popped Ellen heard a slight sound and suddenly found herself once again in the body slumped on the floor of the cave. She sat up straight and glanced at the ceiling.

I can still see them. And as if in answer the tallest Indian, the one who had beckoned from the fire made a gesture toward her, a gesture that said, "You are alive and we are with you."

Caudill straightened from the fire and spoke her name.

"Well, Miss Ellen, did you have a little nap? I like that. Now we can eat and then we can get better acquainted."

Ellen explored the wall and floor with her fingers. Maybe she could hit him with a rock, or a stick.

At each side of the man and at back of him, Ellen could see figures forming... figures bathed in firelight... figures ornamented with feathers and painted designs. He seemed unaware that figures drifted with him toward the open fire.

Then, as she watched, the transparent figures solidified to make a slow dance around the circle of flame.

Merle Caudill looked puzzled at first, then angry.

"Who the hell are you? Where'd you redskins come from?"

The dancers moved more quickly, none speaking, none looking at the oil man, but the circle arched him in toward the central fire.

"What the hell...?" Merle's voice wasn't a shout, but the dance continued, their bodies buffeting the white man closer and ever closer to the fire.

"Who are you? Leave me alone." Then a scream, "Ellen..."

Ellen stood but found she could not move, could only stand and watch as the dancing figures touched the oil man to the flame and out and into the flame again and out. His pained screams echoed into every corner of the cave. Ellen too, found herself screaming, screaming for help, for Roman.

The figures pressed the oil man from every side and held him for seconds in the midst of the fire he had built, his clothing now afire. A long moment passed, then his anguished cries were interrupted by a man bolting from the passageway to throw Caudill to the floor and roll him across the stone to quench the flame. Other men followed and they threw jackets to help put out the human torch. Ellen felt herself go limp with gratitude.

"Roman," she barely breathed the name but the man working with Caudill seemed to hear her. He relinquished his place to one of the other men and raced to put his arms around Ellen.

"Are you hurt, my Ellen?"

"Oh Roman, I'm fine. But there were Indians... they put him in the fire... they were at the ceiling..." Her incoherent speech was muffled against the man's shoulder. "I wanted to hit him."

"Hush now. He is in the care of his own, now. Do not concern yourself."

Ellen peered at the sheriff and another man helping the oil man to move toward the entryway. Caudill babbled and stretched his hands before himself as if her were searching for something that was not there.

Ellen looked up into the smooth tan face, to smile into the dark eyes.

"Roman?" Her question held a million questions.

"Ellen," His answer held all the answers.

A silent shimmering figure floated to touch them and it spoke words Ellen understood but did not know.

"He blessed us, Roman."

"Yes, my Ellen, that is what he did."

Chapter 22

When the sound of Jake's wagon could no longer be heard, Ellen leaned forward to touch Roman's hand. Before her fingers touched him she traced a pattern in the air above the Indian man's palm.

His dark gaze lifted from her hand to her face and Ellen could see a smile in the depth of his brown eyes.

"You haven't forgotten." His hand clasped Ellen's.

She stepped closer to him then laid her forehead upon his broad silk shirted chest. "Feels nice," she murmured.

"Now you know why I wear silk."

"I wasn't talking about your shirt."

His silk covered, muscular arm encircled her shoulders and pulled her close. Again Ellen heard the word spoken over her head, the word that had glittered in the air above her twice before.

"You've got to quit doing that," she whispered, "Either that or you must teach me what to say to you."

"I have quit," his tone was solemn, "We no longer have need for such things, you and I. You are safe and I hold you in my arms," the embrace tightened, "We will be safe with each other, now."

Ellen smiled against the shirt. I won't tell him, she thought, Yahola wants me to keep it a secret. She wound her arms about the man, "We Indian women need to have some things all our own," she told herself.

A long moment passed, then Ellen stepped away from Roman and gestured toward the dark passageway. "Do you think they are watching us?"

"I am sure so."

"I don't see them."

Again he turned the dark smiling gaze down to look into her eyes. "We will not need them." He looked toward the ledge, then back toward the shadows, then into her eyes again. "But they will watch nevertheless."

Ellen smiled. "Well, if they are watching and you are watching, I suppose I won't have any trouble getting out of here."

"I will go first." Roman moved toward the cave opening. You must follow just behind me." His hand lingered in a light caress across Ellen's cheek. "I want you always in my sight, my woman."

Ellen nodded.

"Yes my love, my Roman."

She walked the path toward the light, almost touching Roman. When they stepped outside her eyes needed to acclimate to the sun. She hesitated a moment and looked back at a black skirt that swirled inside, close to the cave opening. With a secret smile Ellen looked at the white shirtwaist and at the peach colored cameo at the throat. Above the cameo, her cousin's face smiled down at her. Yahola lifted her left hand and made a slow movement.

She's waving, she's telling me goodbye.

Ellen lifted her own hand toward the fading figure.

Roman stood waiting for her on the ledge near the pathway.

It almost seems strange, she thought, to be here with no sound, no fire, no drums, no dancers. She smiled again at Roman and he reached for her hand.

"We will go home now," he said, "Our home."

About the Authors

Jackie King is a native Oklahoman whose grandfather Gilbert (Gib) Hodges settled in the Oklahoma Panhandle before statehood.
Web site: **http://www.jacqking.com**

Peggy Moss Fielding is a native of Oklahoma. Her great grandfather, J. W. Fulkerson, made one of the runs into the Territory to plat out the townsite of Fulkerson Camp. The name of the town was later changed to Drumright at her great grandfather's request.
Web site: **http://www.peggyfielding.com**

Printed in the United States
128623LV00002B/7/P